WAIT FOR ME

SOLAR BURN SERIES
BOOK 1

HEATHER CARSON

This book is a work of fiction. Although references to certain locations are present, please allow the creative suspension of reality that was needed to complete this story for your reading pleasure. All characters are entirely fictional. Any resemblance to actual persons living or dead is coincidental.

Table of Contents

1

Tessa

"Mom, I can't find the remote!"

Tessa dropped the laundry basket onto the cedar chest at the foot the king-sized bed. Moose collapsed on the carpet by her feet, huffing as he closed his eyes.

"It was one flight of stairs," Tessa teased the English chocolate lab. "What are you going to do when your dad gets back and drags you out on runs again?" Moose opened one eye and stared at her with his tail thumping at some of his favorite words.

"Mom," Emily's high-pitched whine drifted up the stairs. "The T.V. isn't working and I can't find the remote anywhere."

"Where did you put it last?" Tessa pulled out the faded blue t-shirt with the embossed Navy Corpsman letters stamped across the front that had somehow avoided the washing machine for the past six months. *Three more days.* She smoothed out the wrinkles and folded it against the bed. Three more long days, but then he'd be home from deployment and she was taking a kid-free vacation somewhere. She always said it, but this time she was…

"Mom!"

"I'm coming." Tessa left the unfolded laundry in the basket. Moose groaned as he stood up again and dutifully followed her back down the stairs.

"Did you check the couch cushions?"

"Uh huh." Emily nodded, her red and unruly curls bouncing on her head. "Peppa Pig is gone and I didn't touch any buttons or anything."

"You lost Peppa too?" Tessa's jaw dropped in mock horror.

Belly giggles erupted from the girl. "No. Peppa went away when the man came on T.V."

"Well then let's go see if we can make him go away." Tessa laughed as she reached for her daughter's hand.

Toys littered the light blue and white checkered rug that stretched out across the stone tile floor. It was a miracle they'd found a rental with carpeted bedrooms in Southern California since every builder seemed obsessed with tile. Honestly, it was a miracle they'd found a rental at all in this market. A whole house to clean just to watch your kids destroy it.

"Did you drop it in the toy box when you pulled all this out?"

"I already looked there," Emily said.

"Did you check in the…" Tessa's voice trailed off as she stared at the television screen. The volume was turned down, but the local news anchor sat at his desk, moving his mouth with urgency. A red emergency alert banner ran across the top of the frame with the warning: *This is not a drill. Shelter in place orders are now in effect.*

"Mommy." Emily tugged at her hand. The color drained from Tessa's face as she watched the screen in confusion, trying to make sense of the words.

"Go find the remote."

"But I don't know where it is." Emily stomped her foot on the floor and sent the Barbie dream car flying across the rug until it smacked into a half-naked Ken doll with his arms bent behind his back. Her eyes widened when she realized what she'd done. But Tessa didn't scold her for the tantrum. She moved in a trance to the television and pressed the plus sign for the volume.

"I repeat, Governor Ronan has ordered that all residents are to stay at home until service centers are established. Help will be coming soon for those who need it. Stay off the roads to keep them clear for first responders and aid workers. Jeanie, have we got Doctor Mitchell on the line yet?"

The screen darkened and a loud beeping blared through the house from the television and the phone on the kitchen counter from the national Emergency Alert System explaining that this was, in fact, not a drill and "Stay at home orders are in effect." Emily screamed at the sudden sound, clamping her hands over her ears, and Tessa ran her fingers through the girl's hair to soothe her even as her own heart began to race. The news program returned and her phone buzzed on the counter with its familiar ring.

"Peppa Pig?" Emily asked hopefully as Tessa sprinted toward the kitchen. Landon was with a Marine Expeditionary Unit as a hospital corpsman for his Marines and traveling home by ship from Hawaii. It was the first time in six months she'd left the phone out of reach. He wouldn't call her until they were stateside and got service again. She knew that. Yet, the familiar panic at missing one of his calls sent her sliding in socks across the tile floor and ripping the phone from the charger.

She bypassed the emergency alert notification on the screen, punching the green answer button with the pad of her finger, and barely registered the 208 Idaho area code. *It's not him.* She pressed the box against her ear and ran back to the living room.

"Christ, Tessa. I've called you fifteen times in the past two hours." The gruff voice blasted through the speaker of the phone as the screen on the television split into two, one video with the news anchor adjusting his microphone and the second screen showing a woman in a red blouse who was yanking her hair into a ponytail. *Dr. Mitchell* the credentials at the bottom of her screen said.

"Dad?" Tessa pulled the phone back from her ear, checking the digits again to see the landline number from the sheriff's office.

"I need you to listen to me," he said.

The news anchor stared at the doctor. Tessa focused on her too, ignoring whatever her father was about to say. "Thank you for joining us on such short notice. Can you explain what is happening with this solar flare?"

"It's not just solar flares. The solar flares and extra activity we saw over the past twenty or so hours are what we would normally consider typical if not a bit intense solar storm. This is something different. It's a coronal mass ejection which in the simplest terms is an explosion of plasma and magnetic field from the sun. Our SOHO satellite at Lagrange Point 1 registered the first of the CMEs heading earth's way about three hours ago."

"The first?" The news anchor reached for his handkerchief and wiped the sweat beads off his balding head.

"Yes," Dr. Mitchell continued. "The first blast followed a trajectory that should have missed us, but the second ejection increased the solar wind speed in a southern direction and more than doubled the size of the magnetic storm. The third that followed right behind was too large for our systems to measure. NASA was able to monitor the new direction of all three CMEs before the highly ionized particles shorted out the circuits in the satellite an hour ago and that's the last bit of warning we have. Any minute now we should be seeing the effects of the first event followed shortly by the next two."

"I'm sorry. Can you explain that? How are satellites meant to withstand solar radiation in space damaged by the sun?"

"That's why this is so urgent. We've never seen anything like it. The satellite went off line to protect itself as the storms passed and now we can't get it back on. CMEs aren't supposed to be this strong." Dr. Mitchell's feed froze and the news anchor requested technical support.

"Tessa, are you even listening to me?"

"I'm trying to understand what is going on in the news right now, Dad."

"That's what I've been explaining to you." There was a shuffle as his fist hit the desk, sending papers flying. She could just imagine sitting in the worn green leather chair across from him in his office.

"If you're going to be a jerk, I'm going to hang up."

"Listen to me and please don't hang up. We aren't going to have much time." The sudden softness in his voice disarmed her. It had been years since he'd spoken that way. Not since she was a little girl and her mom left the two of them alone, forcing them to figure out life together which they never could quite do.

"I'm listening." The words were almost painful to speak. But Emily dove into the toybox to search for the remote without complaint and the people on the news who took away Peppa Pig looked like they were about to cry and a sickening form of fear was curling in the pit of her stomach. For once, she was too stunned to argue.

"Have you been watching the news for the past few hours?" His voice changed back to the small-town sheriff roughness, covering up any hint of surprise at the ease of the win.

"I never watch the news when Landon is gone, but I'm watching it right now. They have a shelter in place in effect for this solar storm thing."

"Okay, I need to tell you something and you have to hear what I'm saying. The governor radioed me about thirty minutes ago and said to hold the town on lockdown for the immediate future. Projected estimates are saying to prepare emergency services for weeks to a few months, if not a year. The government is not ready to handle this. No one is. You need to get away from those cities and come back home. Now. Before it gets worse."

"You do remember that you freaked out like this about the pandemic and we handled that just fine. I don't think a solar storm is this big of a deal." Tessa pulled the phone away from her ear and put it on speaker as she opened up the blue app to check social media but the pages wouldn't load.

"This isn't just a solar storm. It's a CME. A Carrington type event. It happened in the 1800's and wiped out the power grid. And it isn't one. It's three of them. I don't think you understand how serious this is. Without power, the world as we know it will not continue to work."

"Was there even power in the 1800's?" Tessa's hand shook as she hit refresh on the feed.

"No jokes," Sheriff Neil growled. "Get the kids out of there and get up here now. You're running out of time."

"Landon will be back in three days. I'll ask him when he gets home if he wants to spend his leave up there, but I don't know what the military is going to do if this is as bad as you say it will be." She swiped again. An image cleared of Amy's son chasing bubbles on the lawn. *Oklahoma springs are gorgeous!! Glad we got stationed here.*

"Are you going to waste the rest of your life waiting on him?"

Her jaw clenched and she almost threw the phone. "Thank you for your concern, but we will be alright."

"Damn your pride." He took a deep breath, and backtracked, "I'm sorry. I shouldn't have said it that way. I don't want anything to happen to you or the kids. Can you come back home where you'll be safe?"

She took the phone off speaker. If he was apologizing to her than the world was really going to end. "I can't just leave without Landon. If I need somewhere to go, we should be safe on base and I'll take the kids there."

"I don't think the base will be safe either soon." Static cut through the line making his voice seem like it was under water. Ribbons of interference broke the news anchor's face into a rainbow of pixels.

"Dad?" Tessa's heart beat faster. "Are you still there?"

"I'm here." The response was too far away.

Emily tugged at Tessa's hand, holding the remote triumphantly in the air. Electricity crackled across the television freezing a pixelated image of the doctor with mascara running from her tear-filled eyes.

"I need to go get Mason from school," she whispered, afraid that speaking out loud would make any of this true.

"Hurry." The word was a warning broken into fragments of sound as the call dropped and the television screen went black.

"Now it's really broken." Emily stood pressing the red power button on the remote over and over again.

Tessa blinked. *This isn't happening.* She swiped at the screen of her phone again trying to pull up the news site on the search engine despite the three dots of no service death in the upper right corner. Nothing loaded. She clicked on her email icon and typed out a quick message to the long chain of responses between her and Landon. *Something is going on with the power. Sorry about earlier. I love you.* The message failed to send. She hit retry and shoved the phone in her back pocket. Anxiety rocked its way through her core. She swallowed hard, trying to think.

"Can you fix it?" Emily stared at her mom, waiting for her to do something to bring Peppa back.

"Not right now." Tessa forced herself to smile. "Good job finding this though. Now go get your shoes on."

She raced through the house hitting the light switches in every room at the top of the stairs and hoping for the familiar warm glow from a single bulb. Each empty click resounded too loud in her ears, the silence pronounced by her panicked breathing and the heavy beat of her heart. *Focus.* She willed herself to slow down.

So what if the power goes out? There were marshmallows and graham crackers in the pantry. Worst case scenario, it'd be like an extended camping trip. *For a year.* Her father's words threatened to break through the resolve she was building. He could be dramatic sometimes. She stood in the darkness of the hallway bathroom. *But he'd actually apologized.*

Pure instinct made her rip back the shower curtain printed with colorful fish and scoop out the toys in the tub. She plugged in the stopper and turned the water on full blast. It poured from the faucet as loud as a geyser in the quiet house.

"Is it bath time?" Emily asked from the open door with her untied shoes on the wrong feet.

"No sweetie." Tessa tried to calm her racing thoughts. "I just want to fill the tubs up for later in case we want some water." *In case we don't have water.* She sucked in a steadying breath and turned to knot the laces on Emily's shoes. "Why don't we fill up all the sinks and then we'll go get your brother?"

Tessa balanced Emily on her hip as she ripped her purse and keys from the hook. She didn't bother to lock the door as they hurried outside. The neighborhood was safe enough and no one messed with them up there on the hill. She glanced up at the brilliant blue sky and the sun shining down on the desert valley. It was like any other day. *Shouldn't it be shooting flames if there was some kind of massive storm?*

"Can I watch a movie?"

"Sure baby." Tessa strapped Emily into her booster seat in the back of the Kia Telluride. She turned the key in the ignition and the engine purred to life. A static pop sent the systems haywire. Lights flashed across the dashboard and the navigation screen displayed a system error. *You've got to be kidding me. This thing is brand new.*

Tessa dropped her hands from the wheel, turning the vehicle off and then back on. The GPS screen remained blank and the check engine light was on, but other than that it all seemed fine. She put the vehicle in reverse and pressed on the gas. The anti-lock braking system light flared up and the tires screeched to a stop. Emily cried out at the sudden jerk. *Of course this is happening right now.*

"New plan." Tessa turned in her seat, reaching for Emily's hand to calm her down. "Mommy's car is a little sick. Can you sit here and be a big girl while I get daddy's truck?" A smile spread across her face as she nodded.

The remote to the garage wasn't working. She tossed it into the Kia and ran back through the house. Moose lifted his head from his nap on the couch as she yanked off the worn throw pillow. "Sorry, boy. I'll be right back," Tessa called to him over her shoulder as she threw open the door. She fumbled in the dark for the dusty release lever hanging from the garage ceiling.

Sunlight filtered into the room as Tessa forced the metal door open until the springs caught hold of it. She stood there panting from the effort, waiting for the thing to come crashing back down. *This is not the end of days.* It's just a power outage and really bad deployment luck with her vehicle. Everything was going to be okay.

She uncovered Old Blue and the sun reflected off the garish cobalt paint of Landon's 1982 Ford F150. The gas guzzler. The money pit. The single cab machine of death that Landon insisted on keeping in mint condition despite Tessa's insistence that it was a dead horse. It roared to life with the spare key on her chain.

"Yes." Tessa pressed her forehead against the steering wheel, breathing a sigh of relief. Last deployment she'd forgotten to start it every few days and the battery was dead when Landon got home. This time she'd been smart. She put the throw pillow on the worn seat and propped it up so she could see over the dashboard.

"Is daddy's truck sick too?" Emily asked as she pushed open the door to the Kia.

"Sure isn't." Tessa left Old Blue running as she ran over to get the booster and install it in the cab of the truck.

"I can't wait for him to come home." Emily leaned against Tessa's side and held up her fingers. "Three more days."

"Three days," Tessa said. And that was it. Only three more chains on the construction paper ribbon that she'd hung above the fireplace. All the tantrums, the late-night tears, the wins and losses she'd dealt with; all the broken Facetimes, dropped calls, and whispered promises in between. The fear, the waiting, tuning out each news alert and pretending the worst couldn't happen to you because that was the only way to survive the kind of life they led. It would all be over soon and they could deal with this solar storm or whatever it was together.

She wouldn't have to do it alone anymore.

Three more days.

She backed out of the driveway and onto the dead-end road at the top of the hill. There was only one other house up on the ridge. The larger property to the right was owned by Alan or Carter, *something like that*, and his wife. She couldn't remember their names. But he was a nice enough old man. He'd spoken with her husband a few times when they first moved in, but then Landon deployed and she hadn't done more than wave when they both happened to be bringing out the trash cans at the same time.

Open fields of dirt and sagebrush dotted with rugged pine trees lined the hill in either direction. It was easy to pretend they lived somewhere rural like their old house in North Carolina until the road made a sharp curve at the base of the hill, spitting them out into a cookie cutter subdivision of newly built houses with shared plastic fences.

Turner Street was blocked by a stalled white Suburban in the middle of the road. A woman with huge Botoxed lips and dyed blond hair stood next to the open driver side door holding her cellphone in the air and calling out to the man in his suit and tie who had the hood of his Hyundai propped open in his driveway. Both of them turned to wave her down when Old Blue's loud engine roared onto the street.

"Are their cars sick too?" Emily asked.

What is happening? Tessa gripped the wheel hard, torn between the desire to help and the overwhelming need to make sure her son would be safe. She maneuvered the truck on to the side walk and cranked the window down as she passed. "I'll be back in a bit."

The woman stuck her middle finger in the air.

"I said I'd be back." She rolled the window up and mumbled what she would have liked to say under her breath so her daughter wouldn't hear.

Emily was already laughing as she bounced along in her car seat. "Can we turn the music on? I want rock-n-roll." Tessa reached for the dial, knowing Landon's station was already tuned in. Nothing, not even static, played back no matter what she did. She pulled her hand to her lap. *If the radio signal was gone and the cellphones weren't working, what did that mean for all communications?*

She focused on what she could control. Once she got Mason and they were safely back home, everything would be okay. The military would have something in place for a disaster like this. Landon will know what to do. *Three more days.* She repeated the words like a mantra.

The onramp for the interstate was a congested mess of stalled cars and vehicles that were on the shoulder trying to get around them. She glanced at the overpass before the hill sloped down. Even if she could get up there, she wouldn't be moving fast. Old

Blue bounced over the median, crushing the bushes under the oversized tires, as she turned to the side road to bypass the traffic. People poked their heads out of businesses, holding their cellphones pointed at the sky and gawking at the commotion on the streets.

"Why is everyone's car sick?" Emily asked as they passed another hood popped open with a frustrated woman trying to jumpstart her battery using a handheld charger. Tessa bit her lip as a motorcycle flew by them in a hurry, weaving around the traffic and stalled vehicles up ahead as if they were practice cones.

"Not all of them are." A Chevy Silverado backed out of the traffic jam and its tires squealed as it flew down the alley with a hard right turn. It felt strange to watch them drive this way, but she made the turn down the alley after the vehicle without a second thought. "Daddy's truck is fine."

"But his music is broken," Emily pointed out in all her infinite wisdom. "Just like the T.V."

"Hey now. It's going to be okay." Tessa glanced at her and smiled. "Remember when we had the hurricane warning last year in the old house and the power went out for a little while. That's all this is."

"Mommy!" Emily screamed.

"Close your eyes." Tessa's hand clamped around her daughter's head, pulling her close to her chest, and she accelerated out of the alley past the open intersection. Power cables danced along the street sending sparks flying that caught with the flames rising from the twisted metal heaps of the collision at the broken light. "Sing me a song, alright?"

Tears burned Tessa's eyes as she drove past the blood-soaked woman who stood sobbing over the charred remains of a body lying on the asphalt. There were no sirens, no flashing blue and red lights, but people were running out from the 7-11 gas station and trying to help pull another man from the metal carnage of what was left of the vehicles.

"A, b, c, d…" Emily's voice shook as she tried to keep singing.

"It's okay now. You can open your eyes." Her knuckles were white as she gripped the steering wheel and she blinked hard to clear her vision.

"Why was that woman bleeding?"

"She was in a car accident." She choked back a sob, praying her daughter hadn't seen the burnt flesh of the body on the ground.

Emily turned her face to the floor and watched her shoes as she bounced them back and forth. The sequins caught glimmers of the sun and reflected them across the dashboard. "I'm really glad that Daddy's truck can't get sick."

Tessa cut through the parking lot of a grocery store to avoid the main street and drove the side road that led to the baseball fields behind the school. Parents were already running along the back fences as they rushed to the front of the building. Their frightened faces tore at a primal fear deep inside of her. *Just get Mason and take the kids home.*

She pulled Old Blue up to where the pickup line normally started, but an empty security car and a line of orange cones had blocked off the entrance. At least there was parking on the street. Tessa backed up and settled the truck in next to the sidewalk. The mob of panicked parents was coming closer. She unbuckled Emily and carried her on her hip as she raced ahead of them.

There was already a crowd in front of the school and they waited, checking their phones for service and standing on tiptoes to see what the holdup was.

"Give me my daughters!" a woman screamed from somewhere near the double glass doors.

"If you wait your turn in line, ma'am, we'll get them out in a minute," the principal tried to placate her.

"Maggie, Katie," the woman continued, ignoring him. "Mama's here. Come on outside." The crowd shifted anxiously. The anger in the woman's voice ignited their own fear and lips pressed together in thin lines, each parent struggling with whether to lash out in panic like the crazed mother up front was doing or to wait for word on what was going on.

"If you'll all just form a single file line on the sidewalk, we'll release each student individually." Principal Mossley remained calm despite the shrieking.

"Maggie! Katie!"

Emily buried her face against Tessa's shoulder and Tessa stepped into line with the rest of the parents.

"Don't you dare touch me." The woman jumped from the curb and away from the principal's outstretched hand. Her normally perfect braid was coming undone and wild hair billowed around the face of the PTO leader Tessa had heard speak at the last meeting, but she struggled to remember her name.

"Sharon, please get yourself together," Principal Mossley tried to reason. "You're causing a scene."

"Give me my daughters." Sharon's face twisted into a snarl as she lunged past the security officer who stood shoulder to shoulder with the principal.

"Mommy!" Two little girls with matching ribbons tied into their pigtails came skipping through the open doors. Sharon paused long enough to wrap her arms around them and glanced over at the other parents who were trying to avert their gaze.

"You're all sheep. You are never going to survive this." Sharon spit as she guided her girls away.

Tessa let the words roll off of her and tried to keep them from burrowing too deep in her mind. She wasn't a sheep, but she wasn't going to lash out right now and scare her children.

"Why was she screaming like that?" Emily whispered.

Tessa adjusted her weight so Emily was seated on her arm. "She's just scared. People do dumb things when they are afraid."

That's what your dad always said. Tessa pushed the thought away. He never trusted anyone because he was the sheriff of a small town. It was a requirement of the job or something. But she knew that was his biggest fear. Too many people in one area and what they could do to each other if they were afraid. The parent behind her pushed too close to her back and Tessa's whole body tensed. *Just breathe.* Everything would be okay once she got the kids back home.

The line moved forward until she was standing in front of Principal Mossley. "Mason Ward is my son. He's in 2nd grade. Mr. Bank's class."

"Mason Ward," he turned to call out to the security officer. Yellow sweat stained his shirt collar and the principal didn't meet her eyes. He was scared too and she felt the sudden need to help in some way.

"Thank you for protecting our kids and I'm sorry you had to deal with that. You're a great principal." He gave her a tired smile and motioned to the next person in line.

"Hey, Mom." Mason raced out of the doors and came up to meet her on the sidewalk.

"Mason," Emily shrieked as she wiggled out from her mother's arms and wrapped her brother in a tight hug.

Relief coursed through her when she saw his gap-toothed smile and messy head of brown hair that seriously needed to be cut. His collectable keychains bounced against his spiderman backpack as he jumped up and down.

"The whole school is dark. It was so cool. You should have seen it when everyone screamed. Mr. Bank gave us an extra recess."

"Sounds cool." Tessa reached for their hands.

A burly man wearing a Metallica t-shirt with the sleeves ripped off shoved his way through the back of the line that had formed all the way to the fence. "I'm not waiting to get my kid. Willow!"

"Let's go." Tessa pulled her children through the parking lot and past the orange cones to get them away from whatever crazy scene was coming next.

"Old Blue." Mason pumped his fist in the air when he saw the truck. "Is Dad home already?"

"Not yet." Tessa hesitated, pushing her kids behind her back. *Did I forget to close that?* The driver side door was open. She reached for the passenger handle and pulled it towards her. A woman with stringy black hair and bloodshot eyes froze, staring up at her from under the steering wheel column with a screwdriver in her hand.

"What do you think you're doing? Get the hell out of my truck."

The woman glanced at the screwdriver and Tessa lunged forward, clawing under the seat for the hatchet Landon always kept there. Her pulse raced as her fingers slipped over the jumper cables and enclosed around the steel handle. She yanked it free in

24

a solid sweep, holding it above her head like a battle ax. "I said go."

The woman staggered backwards. Her dilated pupils were fixed on the dull and rusty blade. She raised her hands into the air. "My bad. I thought this was my friend's truck. Same color and all."

Tessa didn't move until the woman had retreated across the street and then she scrambled into the truck, pulling the kids in behind her and slamming the doors shut before locking them.

"Who was that, Mom?" Mason stared at the hatchet still clenched in her fist. She dropped it to the floorboard and kicked it beneath the seat. Her hands shook as she reached over to buckle Emily's strap.

"Just some crazy lady," Tessa whispered. "Get your seatbelt on."

Emily turned to smile at her older brother, happy he was home and proud to have some inside knowledge about the changing world that he didn't yet understand. "Don't worry. It will be okay. But it's better if you don't look."

The drive home took over an hour. Tessa avoided the main streets as much as possible, taking the long route along the mountain side that wrapped back under the freeway. She'd cursed Old Blue more times than she cared to admit over the years, but when she needed the four-wheel drive to climb the sandy hill on the backside of the weigh station and get around the stalled semi-truck that had no business being on that road, she lovingly caressed the steering wheel and whispered, "Thanks."

The Suburban was still blocking Turner Street but the blond driver was nowhere in sight. She slowed down, scanning the houses of her neighbors in the subdivision and tried to see if she could find out where the woman might be. No one stepped from their doors or peeked from their windows and there were no kids playing on the lawns so she eased Old Blue onto the sidewalk and continued up the hill. Mason and Emily were still cracking up about the bumpy ride when she pulled into the garage and turned the key.

"Stay here for just a second." She smiled at them.

Mason stopped laughing and arched his eyebrow, looking so much like Landon that it hurt to breathe. "Is there a surprise we aren't supposed to see?"

"Something like that." Tessa shut the door and crouched down with her back pressed against the truck until she was lower than the window. Tremors racked her body and she clutched her hands over her mouth to muffle the wordless scream. It had only been a couple of hours and the world already looked like this. What was going to happen a few days from now if they didn't get the power back on? *How can I protect them?* She rubbed her hands over her eyes, wiping away the tears. *You don't have another choice.* The power would be back on soon. They just needed to pass the time. She inhaled deeply and nodded once to confirm.

"Alright guys." She opened the door, sweeping her arm in a grand gesture as her children waited in anticipation for the big surprise to come. "Who wants hot dogs and smores over the campfire for dinner tonight?"

Moose came racing through the house to greet his humans with his nails clacking across the tile floor and his bushy tail wagging in the air. Mason shrugged off his backpack and dropped to one knee to get a sloppy lick as Emily ran to the living room to grab the remote. Tessa went to the pantry and then to the cupboard, scanning each package of food and mentally calculating how long the dried goods would last and how many meals she could make out of it all.

After the hurricane warnings in North Carolina, she'd made it a habit to keep a few weeks' worth of food on hand just in case. Then there were Landon's favorites. She'd hit the grocery stores yesterday to stock up for his homecoming so they wouldn't have to go shopping on his precious few days of post-deployment leave. There were good steaks in the freezer and the beer fridge in the garage was full. All the essentials were accounted for.

The sink gurgled and Tessa turned in panic, rushing over to rip the stopper from Mason's hand and shove it back into place.

"What?" Mason asked, with his head cocked to the side. "The water is just sitting there."

"We need it." She turned on the faucet and a steady stream poured out. "Actually, go do me a favor and grab some buckets from the garage."

"But it's dark in there," Mason whined. Tessa rummaged through the junk drawer and pulled out a couple of flashlights, handing one to him with a smile. "Fine," he mumbled as he flicked on the beam. "But you promised we were having smores."

With the buckets and every available jug to hold water filled and the faucet still running, the tension in her shoulders eased a little. She opened the pantry to pull out the peanut butter and graham crackers. Moose huffed as he settled into his usual place on the rug in front of the sink to guard the stove.

"Sorry buddy." She pulled the hotdogs from the fridge and quickly shut the door. "No cooking scraps tonight."

The kids were out back playing on their swing set and waiting for Tessa to start the fire. She switched on the flashlight. The beam wavered as she aimed it into the garage and she hit the plastic side against the palm of her hand to steady the light. She'd have to round up batteries in the morning if the power still wasn't on. At least the beer fridge was cold. All the bottles perfectly lined up to fill the shelves. She grabbed one and twisted off the top. Landon wouldn't mind. She needed it today.

"Finally." Mason launched himself off the swing and landed on two feet in the dirt. "I'm so hungry I could eat a whole cow."

"Yeah, well I'm so hungry I could eat a whole… whole," Emily's voice trailed off as she looked around the fenced backyard, "house!"

Tessa set down the food and beer on the glass patio table. Mason had already dragged a stack of wood over to the fire pit.

"And I'm so hungry that I could eat two little kids." She turned to growl and they both screamed as they darted out of reach.

"Again, Mommy!"

Dusk arrived slowly and with it came tendrils of red and bright orange cloudlike whisps that were nowhere near the setting sun. The light danced over the mountains in the distance where the sky should already be turning dark blue. Tessa stared at the sun and wished it would go away already. It'd done enough damage for the day.

As darkness continued to fall, the trails of light burned brighter casting an angry glow over the night and blocking out the stars of the never-ending desert sky. She'd seen glimpses of the aurora borealis growing up in Idaho winding above the tree branches, but never this ominous and unforgiving. It wasn't soft in the way light should be. It was harsh and dangerous and loud. The smoke from the fire drifted lazily towards the sky as she stoked the embers.

"This is crazy." Mason stole glances at the light show above them as he reached for the marshmallow bag with sticky fingers and a smear of chocolate across his cheek. "Can I have one more?"

"Last one."

Emily's breathing grew steady and even as she dozed on Tessa's lap. Tessa moved slowly so as not to wake her, smearing the peanut butter onto a graham cracker and breaking off a piece of chocolate to nestle into the spread. Mason blew at the flaming ball of marshmallow.

"Dad always makes them golden." Mason frowned at the charred mess.

"I like them a little burnt." Tessa used the top cracker to ease the marshmallow onto the sandwich and then handed it to him. "But he'll be home soon and can show you how to get them just right."

"You think it looks like this everywhere? Is Dad seeing the same thing?" Mason chewed thoughtfully as he stared at the sky. The warm orange glow shining off his face had nothing to do with the fire. It was strange to look at him in this light. He was still a little boy, but his baby chub was long gone and he acted older when he wanted to. *He's just like Landon.*

"I don't know, sweetheart. Guess we'll ask him when he gets here. But hurry up and finish so we can go wash your face and get you both into bed."

3
Landon

"Hey, Doc. Wake up."

The curtain on his rack was pulled to the side. Landon groaned and forced his eyes open in the bright fluorescent light as he glared at the Marine. "What is it now?"

"Martinez is losing it. I need you to go check him out." Sergeant Sierra shrugged.

"I can't deal with anymore vomit. I've been up for two days straight handling this bug you've all been spreading around. Just send him to medical to get some Imodium." Landon rubbed his hands over his face, trying to wake up. Being the Navy Corpsman in a unit of Marines was a lot like dealing with toddlers. *So much for going to sleep early.*

"He's not sick like that." Sgt. Sierra offered a half-hearted smile. "I know you had a late night, but I don't know what else to do."

"It's always a late night. Can't you guys just stop being idiots for three more days until we get home?" Landon yawned as he jumped down from his rack and then opened his locker to pull out his boots.

"About that," Sgt. Sierra paused before they made their way out of the berthing, "word is navigation is down and we're not going home just yet. That's why Martinez is all worked up."

Landon closed his eyes. They couldn't do this to him now. He'd been knee deep in vomit and excrement for the past forty-eight hours, taking care of his unit who'd been hit with viral gastroenteritis during the port call in Hawaii. There wasn't even a spare second to respond to Tessa's last message. She was going to be so mad when she heard they would be delayed.

"You alright, Doc?" Sgt. Sierra glanced over his shoulder.

"Yeah." Landon swallowed hard, twisting the silicone wedding band on his finger. "Where is Martinez at?"

Lance Corporal Martinez. Aged 23. First tour of duty. Lives on base. Pregnant wife. History of anxiety. Two colds in the past year. Landon ran through all the mental notes he could remember about the Marine as he walked the passageways to the medical bay. *Asked for the chaplain's email last month. Requested a light duty chit for a bruised knee.* He added in as much detail from their previous encounters as he could to form the full picture in his head.

"HM2 Ward." The hospital corpsman assigned to the ship and standing duty jumped from her seat as Landon entered the hatch to the main medical compartment.

"HN Rodcliff." He nodded in her direction. "You have one of my guys here?"

"I moved him to the back room," Rodcliff stuttered. "It's after sick call and Commander Jenkins is in a meeting. I just wanted to keep him comfortable until we can sort things out."

"Alright." Landon sighed. "I'm going to check on him."

He pushed open the hatch to the dimly lit room with patient beds reserved for overnight stays. "Hey Martinez. What's going on?"

"Doc." Martinez sat up straight, clutching the thin pillow in his fist. "I can't do this anymore. I need to go home."

"Lay down and let's talk for a minute." His eyes swept over the patient taking a quick visual assessment of outward physical symptoms. Bloodshot eyes, clenched teeth, shaking limbs. "Are you feeling alright?"

LCpl Martinez tossed the pillow aside and swung his legs off the bed, gripping the side of the mattress instead. Tears filled his eyes. "We're headed back to Hawaii and no one knows what's happening. How long are they going to keep us in this steel cage? I have to get out of here."

Hawaii? Landon remained stoic and calm. "This isn't the first time a homecoming has been delayed and I can guarantee you it won't be the last. It's all a part of the job. Just hold tight like the rest of us and we'll get home soon."

34

"My wife is due any day now and they wouldn't give me leave. They wouldn't let me fly off the ship. I can't miss his birth," Martinez spoke too fast.

"Your first?" Landon squatted down so he was eye level with the Marine, trying to recall all the details of the physical assessment he'd given him before they shipped out. He was gushing about being a dad then. Torment played across Martinez's wide eyes as he nodded, trying hard not to let the tears spill out.

"I have two," Landon continued. "My boy Mason is seven and my daughter Emily is four. I missed her birth by two days just like half of the dads on this ship have done. But you can't worry about what you might miss, if that even happens, worry about the years you'll need to be there in the future when he remembers his father's name."

"But Gabrielle is so scared." Martinez broke; his shoulders heaved as he wept openly in the empty patient room. "She needs me to be there for her."

Landon coughed to clear the emotion building in his chest. "She'll understand. Your wife and your unborn son need you to provide for them and your unit needs you here too. I promise this is only temporary. We are going home."

"How's Martinez doing?" Sgt. Sierra leaned against the bulkhead in the corridor outside of medical.

"I had Rodcliff run to get Commander Jenkins and prescribe him an emergency script of hydroxyzine to stop the panic attack. She's going to keep an eye on him while he takes a nap. He should be fit for duty when he wakes up, but he's going to need to follow up with psych when he gets home." Landon twisted the band around his ring finger. "I think he's done after this tour. He doesn't want to stay in."

"The kid is smarter than we ever were then." Sgt. Sierra tapped Landon on his chest. "We should have gotten out and gone to college too. Now look at us. But why does he need to go to the wizard? I thought you were our shrink."

"Let me add that to my list of quals," Landon smirked. "Doc, condom dispenser, baby sitter, psychiatrist. I think I need a pay raise."

"You and me both, brother." Sgt. Sierra laughed. "Can you believe they are doing this though? How hard is it to navigate back to the states without equipment? It's a straight shot east. Big land mass. Can't miss it."

"I know." Landon shook his head as he adjusted his ring back into place. "Hey, I'll catch up with you later. I've got to send an email."

This is the worst time to tell you this… Landon pressed delete until the screen was blank. He sighed, running his hand over his freshly trimmed hair. *Hey beautiful. I'm sure you know by now about the quick delay. I*

*know this is hard, but I love you more than you can imagine.
I'm sorry I didn't reply earlier, things have been a little messy
around here. But I know we need to talk about what you said.
Let's do something together, just me and you, when I get home.*

He read through the email twice, wishing he
was better with words and wanting to wipe the whole
message away. He just needed to hold her in his arms
again. Her fiery red hair getting tangled in the stubble
on his chin, the feel of her shoulders relaxing as she
melted against him. Her pouty lips pressed against his
as her hazel eyes looked up, imploring. Landon hit
send and took a steadying breath. *They'd get through this.
They always did.*

The message failed to send.

Cursing his luck, he copied the text and
pasted it into a new message, that also failed to send.
That's just great. He shoved the keyboard across the
desk and then pulled it back, trying a final time before
exiting out of the browser. But he wasn't fast enough
to not see the message failure error screen. Frustrated,
he made his way to the gym.

Rock notes blared through his earbuds
drowning out the metallic whir of the treadmill under
his feet. He closed his eyes as he ran and focused on
the lyrics, blowing out measured breaths to help him
keep the pace. When his heart was about to explode,
he hit stop and moved to the empty weight bench.
Whoever was there last didn't rerack the weights.
100lbs sat on the bar. Landon added 80lbs more and

pressed until his muscles screamed. The playlist turned to a haunting melody, songs that reminded him of late nights and drinking beer around the firepit.

He blew sweat from his lips as he set the bar and hoisted himself up. The song was too much. He killed the music and wiped his face with the moisture wicking towel, breathing heavily until his heart rate returned to normal. The silence of the gym was foreign, but a welcome escape from the demands of his job that never seemed to end. He sat there a moment longer, enjoying it. Then he put away all the weights and wiped down the equipment.

The shower's hot spray streamed down his back and eased the tension from his muscles. He forced his mind to stay blank, tried not to worry about anything. There was nothing he could do to fix things at home now and he'd learned a long time ago not to focus on what could make you go crazy. This wasn't the first time his job had messed with his marriage. Tessa would understand. *Wouldn't she?* Landon pressed his forehead against the cool steel of the shower stall.

"Hey Doc." The metal rings slid across the bar as the plastic shower curtain was pulled to the side behind him. He turned the water off, glaring over his shoulder. Sgt. Sierra tossed him his towel. "Have you been up topside today?"

"I haven't even had a chance to shower in two days." Landon wrapped the towel around his waist.

"I was wondering what stunk." Sgt. Sierra smirked, but there was something uneasy about his smile. "Get your clothes on and come check this out."

The heavens stretched across the entire world when you stood on the flight deck of the ship and they only touched down at the distant horizon where the sky met the sea. *But this…* This wasn't normal. Landon's eyes widened, reflecting the ghostly trail of red and orange light streaking through the black sky as if the night itself was on fire and reaching down to swallow the ship. He'd seen the aurora borealis growing up in Idaho, the greens and pale yellows that twisted like smoke through the atmosphere, so he knew what he was looking at.

Except this wasn't anything like it at all. The sky was so bright it illuminated the crystal-clear tropical waters beneath the ship making them shine with a bloodied reflection of the galaxy. It was too bright to be the dead of night, and the northern lights shouldn't be at this latitude. Up ahead, the shadowed dark green mountains of Hawaii were lit up by the hellish glow of red clouds dancing around the dormant volcanic peaks and the harbor was littered with thousands of stranded boats, bobbing on the gentle waves and going nowhere.

"Do you have service?" a sailor whispered to someone else, too awestruck to speak out loud. But his words set off a frenzy as everyone pulled out their phones and held them in the air. Landon yanked his own phone from his pocket. If they were this close to land, he might be able to get in touch with Tessa.

He swiped past the lock screen photo of the four of them posed at the dock on a lake and punched in his passcode. There were three dots where bars should be and no Wi-Fi service. He powered his phone off and restarted it, glancing around at the frantic faces that were all trying to do the same. *Hey beautiful. Back in Hawaii. I'll give you a call when I can.* The message lit up with a red exclamation mark as it failed to send.

Landon looked up at the sky again, shielding his eyes from the intensity with his hand and watching the brilliant celestial display as a sick feeling of dread snaked its way down his throat and buried itself in his gut. He knew before the 1MC cackled to life that this was really, really bad.

"General Quarters, General Quarters," the commanding officer barked into the microphone. "All hands below deck now. This is not a drill."

"Doc? Am I covered in radiation or something?" Cpl. Hemming tore at his blouse, his fingers shaking as he fumbled with the buttons. Landon looked to the others, assessing for the first signs of radiation sickness. Boils, burns, vomiting…

All he saw was terrified Marines gathered around him in the hanger bay. Whispered words of "terrorist attack" and "EMP" ran through the crowd. The silent ones with five o'clock shadows on their faces shifted anxiously, waiting to be sent out to fight but not yet knowing what was happening or how they were supposed to fix the bloodthirsty looking sky.

"Keep your uniform on, Corporal," Gunnery Sergeant Fuimaono barked out the order in his heavy accent. The man stood a foot taller than anyone in the room and directed his stern gaze to Hemming as he marched through the crowd. "No one wants to see your hairless chest. Not even Doc." Nervous laughter echoed through the hanger bay as GySgt. Fuimaono made his way to the front of the group.

"It seems we have a problem here, Marines. Looks like the sun has thrown a fit and spit some fireballs at us or whatever the scientists are calling it— ask those rich boys what the technical term is. Best we can tell, it's causing some serious damage. But we've seen worse than this in our lives." GySgt. Fuimaono tensed his muscles, his broad shoulders and heavy biceps stretching the seams of his cammies. It had the intended effect. The Marines all widened their stances, preparing for the moto speech to follow, but Landon had seen this kind of bravado too many times and was tired of these speeches.

"Comms and NAV are down right now, but our Navy boys will get them working soon." GySgt. Fuimaono glanced over to Landon like he had any clue about how a ship should work and hadn't been greenside his entire career. "We're not heading back out. There's nothing for you to fight unless you want to join the Space Force and shoot some plasma back at the sun. The CO is going to make an announcement soon, but I know how trigger happy you all get. Go back to your berthing and sit tight. We'll be home in a few days and you can push Jody out of your bed then."

The "ooh-rah, Gunnys" were tainted with good natured laughter as GySgt. Fuimaono made his way back through the crowd. They formed a respectful path for the legend to pass them by. Technically, he wasn't a god. But the Samoan warrior who towered over any normal man and crushed skulls with his fists came pretty close to one. Everyone had heard the rumors. Smoke pit fairy tales made you infamous. If Gunny said that everything was okay, then it was good enough.

"HM2 Ward." GySgt. Fuimaono paused in front of Landon. His looked down at him from the corner of his eye. "Senior Chief Miller wants all the line corpsman in main medical now."

"Aye Gunny." Landon turned on his heel to leave.

Trepidation slithered down his spine as he made his way back through the corridors and passageways. His thumb brushed against the silicone band for reassurance. *Solar storms couldn't do that much damage, could they?* The ship speakers blasted static throughout the steel walls, stopping Landon in his tracks.

"Attention all hands, stand by for words from the commanding officer." There was a brief pause where it seemed the ship itself held its breath.

"Good evening sailors and Marines. I know everyone is confused as to why we are back in Hawaii. From the intelligence we can piece together via morse code from the surrounding ships, at 0900 this morning solar activity caused a breakdown in communications that seems to stretch over the Pacific. Our ships are hardened for an event like this, but all satellite and radio communications are offline at this point. IT is working to solve a few more glitches to our systems and then we'll be on our way home. I understand this is hard to hear, but we have a job to do and let's not forget it. Mission first."

The echo of his words hung in the stale air long after the 1MC turned off. Landon shook his head. Gunny's speech was better.

Senior Chief Miller stood with his shoulders hunched as if he was crushed by the weight of the air in the room. To be fair, he always looked like that. Salty and worn, like he should have retired years ago.

HM3 Cooper nudged Landon with his elbow as he lowered his head to fit through the hatch. "Can you believe this crap? Just a few more days and we would have been free." Landon stood beside him in silence, not bothering to find another spot. Cooper had a big mouth and an annoying habit of drinking so much in port that he had to be carried in, but his Marines loved him so that had to count for something.

"I think that's everyone." Chief Elyse nodded to the door. Her perfectly filed fingernails drummed against the sleeve of her uniform.

Senior Chief Miller rubbed the back of his neck. "You're all wondering why you're here and wanting to know how serious this solar flare thing is. From everything we are gathering, it doesn't seem anyone was prepared for an event of this magnitude. I can't tell you any more than speculation, but it's going to be a different America we return to. In the coming days, while the ship gets fixed and sets its course back to the states, rumors are bound to run rampant. From a medical standpoint, expect high levels of anxiety if not outright panic from your Marines and any sailors you know on this ship. Most of them will do their jobs, be on the lookout for those who can't handle the stress. If fear begins to spread, mark my words-there will be chaos. Keep your Marines safe and watch out for them. That shouldn't be too hard, right?"

A few chuckles sounded around the room. Landon's fist clenched at his sides, reading the message behind the Senior Chief's words. *Panic. Chaos.* He had to get home and make sure they were alright.

"Are we clear on this?" Chief Elyse stepped forward; her five-foot-four frame commanding the attention of the lower enlisted gathered around. "Your Marines are your responsibility."

"They always were, Chief." Landon sighed.

She narrowed her eyes at him. "Good. Then there should be no issues. Dismissed."

HM3 Cooper sided up next to him as they walked the tight passageway to their berthing. "Something feels off about this. Why would they have that type of meeting?"

Landon forced his shoulders to relax. He felt it too, but he had to maintain his composure for all their sakes. His thoughts drifted to LCpl Martinez. He needed to check on him. "It's probably no big deal. Seeing the sky like that and comms being down right before we are supposed to go home is bound to set everyone on edge. It was more of a preemptive talk so they can't say they didn't warn us."

"Nah, man. I think this is bigger than they are letting on. I don't know that we are going home any time soon." His voice was strong, but he glanced at Landon nervously.

"Don't say that." Landon clenched his jaw. "Don't contribute to the panic. We'll get home one way or another. Just keep your head down and do your job. You don't get paid to think."

4
Tessa

Sometime in the middle of the night Emily had crawled into bed next to Tessa. With the morning sun creeping through the lace curtains, she pried herself from the girl's warm nest of blankets and instinctively reached for her phone. Still no service and only one bar of battery life left even though she'd plugged it into the charger before she fell asleep.

Reality slapped her across the face. The power still wasn't on. *You need to make a plan.* The ache of loneliness crept into the room as it always did at moments like this. She wanted to talk to her husband. What were other people doing? She missed her friends in North Carolina even though they'd all been scattered to the wind. It wasn't like she could call anyone anyway right now.

Moose whined, excited for breakfast, and put his paw on her knee. She scratched behind his ear and drew comfort from his warmth. *The world is not ending.* Humans lived without power for centuries. They'd find a way to survive. She needed to make food for the kids and think of a way to entertain them for the day. The laundry basket was still full of clean clothes that needed to be put away. There were things that had to be done.

She picked up the single folded shirt from the basket and put it on the shelf in Landon's closet above his gun safe. *That needs to be dusted off.* Sighing, she tiptoed out of the room and pressed her finger against her lips as Moose's tail thumped on the floor. With any luck, the kids would sleep in and she'd have some time to herself to figure it all out.

There was still enough coffee left in the pot for a single serving of day-old room temperature caffeine. She drank it straight as she sat perched on the stool for the breakfast counter with a notebook spread before her.

In the right column she wrote down a list of everything they owned that she thought would be useful *if* the world was really ending. They had camping supplies, hiking gear, and enough fuel for the grill to last a while. She would have to check the garage and see what else they had. There was enough food to last at least a few weeks, but a large portion of that was perishable. *If* the power wasn't back on in a few hours then she needed to clear out the fridge somehow.

"Morning Mom." Mason yawned as he padded barefoot into the kitchen. His pajama top was stretched thin, exposing his belly. It'd either shrunk in the wash or the kid wouldn't stop growing. He set the flashlight on the counter. "This isn't working anymore. What's for breakfast?"

Batteries Tessa wrote under the section of things they were going to need and closed the notebook before he could read it. "I don't know yet. Let's see what we've got."

She opened the refrigerator door quickly so as not to let the cold escape and grabbed a handful of things. The bananas and apples could go on the counter. She sniffed the carton of eggs and the package of bacon. *Good enough.* They'd have to use up all the dairy soon, but when Landon got back, she'd go to the grocery store. And if the stores were closed, maybe the local farmer's markets would set up their stalls. It'd be just like the olden times again *if* the power didn't come back on.

The box of matches was in the drawer and she fished them out to light the burner on the gas stove. Moose's eyes followed Tessa's movements as he laid on his favorite rug by the sink. The smell of sizzling bacon filled the kitchen. She paused with the spatula in the pan of scrambled eggs. If the power didn't come back on, how would she get any money out of the bank to buy milk?

One step at a time. She inhaled deeply, pushing the panic away. *Let's just get through the next two days.*

"Breakfast is ready," she called up the stairs. Emily didn't respond. Moose followed on Tessa's heels as she climbed the steps, huffing in indignation that anyone in their right mind wouldn't get up for bacon.

48

"Hey sweetie." She climbed onto the bed and reached over to smooth the messy curls that were frizzed up against the pillow. "Time to get up."

Emily didn't move. Tessa's hand instinctively went to her forehead and she leaned over to get a better look at her face. She wasn't warm, but her eyes were wide open as she stared at the window. Tessa laid down, pulling Emily into her arms and worrying that the crash scene yesterday had already done severe damage but not wanting to bring it up first. *Would she have nightmares for the rest of her life? Be afraid to drive?* No wonder she'd snuck into her bed last night.

"What if Daddy's ship gets sick?" Emily whispered against Tessa's chest.

"Is that what you're worried about? Daddy's ship isn't a car and it seems like only some cars get sick." Tessa ran her fingers in circles against the girl's back, breathing in the soft and almost faded baby scent of her daughter until Emily pulled herself away and sat up. She brushed the wild strands of hair out of her face.

"Okay. But I don't want eggs."

"Tough luck." Tessa rolled her eyes.

A knock at the door sent Moose into a panic, barking as he flew down the stairs. The sharp sound in the quiet house made Tessa's heart jump in her chest.

"Don't answer it," she screamed to Mason as she raced down the steps, imagining the worst. Nothing good ever comes from an unwarranted knock.

"The cops are here," Mason called over his shoulder as he munched on a strip of bacon. Moose bounded through the open door, excited for the intrusion. The color drained from Tessa's face, but she forced herself to slow down and walk steadily forward. If something had happened to Landon, they wouldn't have sent the police. It would be a service member standing at her door. She motioned for the kids to sit at the table and pulled Moose inside by his collar.

"What can I do for you today, Officer…" she scanned his uniform for the gold plate, "O'Brien?"

"Good morning, Miss. Sorry to disturb you, but we're going house to house providing assistance today and asking some questions about your needs." His mirrored sunglasses reflected her image in them. She ran her fingers through her knotted hair and leaned her head past him to see beyond the side of the garage. The cop car was parked in the middle of the road and his partner was walking toward her neighbor's house.

She stepped through the door, closing it behind her, and crossed her arms over her chest to hide the fact that she wasn't wearing a bra. "We don't need any help, but how serious is this if the police are going door to door?"

"I'm not here to cause panic." He pulled a notepad from his pocket. "There's a shelter set up at the high school and another one at United Methodist on Ashwood Avenue if you need food or water or medicine."

She bit her lip. "Are the stores not open?"

"We had to secure local business for now after the riots last night at the grocery stores, but it's under control and nothing to worry about."

"Riots?"

"Like I said, it's under control. If you are in need of food, the shelters will be distribution centers and they are also housing people who need help. They have generators set up providing electricity." He dug in his pants pocket for a pen. "We can give you a ride there now if you want it."

She stared at him in disbelief. "I'm not going to any shelter."

"That's your choice." He sighed. It didn't seem like the first time he'd heard that response today. "How many of you are in this residence? I saw two kids and obviously you, is there anyone else that lives here? Anyone who needs special assistance?" He held the pen above the notepad.

"We don't need any help." She shook her head. "And my husband lives here too."

A heavy black eyebrow arched above the sunglasses. "Your husband. Where is he now?"

Crap. She hated that question and the fear that always came when a stranger asked about their life. Badge or not, there was never a way to tell who you could really trust. "He went to buy some milk, but since the stores are closed, I'm sure he'll be back soon."

"You have a working vehicle?" Officer O'Brien scribbled some words onto the page.

Something felt odd about the urgency in this question.

Tessa didn't miss a beat. "Nope. Our Kia is acting strange so Landon rode his bike down the hill." The sunglasses reflected the Telluride still parked on the street as he turned his head.

"I see." He drew a line through the note. "Two kids. Two adults. No medical issues. And you don't want our assistance right now, which is fine." He lowered the sunglasses so she could see his deep brown and red rimmed eyes. They were lined with bags from a night with no sleep, but seemed to stare straight through her with a sharpness that could only come from years on the job. "Do you own any firearms, registered or otherwise?"

She felt bad for the cop, she really did. How many houses would he have to go to today and deal with worried people who needed help? He seemed like a decent enough guy even though her dad had warned her that city cops weren't worth a damn. At least he wasn't highway patrol.

"Oh no." Tessa put her hand over her heart. "Why would I own any guns? I wouldn't want them around my kids." It was only half a lie. She'd never personally purchased any weapons. That was Landon's thing.

"Alright." He pushed the glasses up the bridge of his nose. "If you have any issues, come down to one of the shelters."

"Will do," she nodded to appease him, "but if I promise not to panic, can you let me know what I should be expecting?"

"Well, if you have some food I wouldn't worry right now. Water may get tricky especially with you being up here on the hill. Gravity can only move it so far without the reservoir pumps working, but you should be okay with what's in the pipes for another day or two. After that, I'd ask your neighbors down the hill if they can let you use the hose."

She wasn't sure if he was purposefully avoiding the real question. "You're expecting this to last a few days then?"

"Maybe a week or so. We'll let you know more when we do." He gave her a tight-lipped smile as he turned away and she knew he was lying too. *A year,* her dad's warning ran through her mind.

She went to the edge of the walkway and watched as O'Brien climbed into the driver side of the patrol car. His partner was shaking his head as he hurried away from the neighbor's house. The old man stood on his porch, barely visible behind the manicured hedges. She still couldn't remember his name. He turned as if he felt her staring at him and she gave an embarrassed wave before rushing inside and bolting the door behind her.

"When Mommy says not to open the door, I mean it." Tessa put her hands on Mason's shoulder and squatted down so she was at eye level with him in his chair.

His cheeks were full of half chewed bacon. "You lied to the cops."

"It wasn't a lie. It was an omission."

"No." He swallowed painfully hard. "You said Dad was home and he isn't. You lied."

"Well he's going to be home soon, so I fibbed a little to make sure the cop wasn't worried about us, okay?" She hoped she sounded convincing. "But when I say not to open the door, don't open the door. Got it?"

"Got it." Mason nodded as he shoveled a forkful of food into his mouth.

"How many bites do I have to take?" Emily pushed the eggs around on her plate. Moose laid under her chair, standing guard to protect the floor from any falling bits of food. It was all so normal that it seemed surreal. *How can there be riots in the grocery stores and shelters set up in town when my kid is still complaining about breakfast?*

"All of the bites." Tessa slumped down on the chair and grabbed a piece of bacon.

She gathered up the dishes from the stove and carried them to the sink. It was amazing how quiet the house had become in less than twenty-four hours with no television noise in the background and without the soft hum of electricity as the appliances did their thing. She reached for the faucet absentmindedly, thinking about what arts and crafts she could scrounge up to keep the kids busy this morning.

No. She turned the handle back and forth, pressing it as far as it would go. The single drop of water that dripped from the faucet made a soft *thud* as it splashed against the metal sink.

Okay. Don't panic. Tessa took a step back. There were four five-gallon buckets of water next to the side door and the counter to the right was covered with jugs and bottles that she'd filled last night. *You should have given the kids a bath.* Both tubs were still full upstairs and she hadn't wanted to empty them yet. At least she'd had the foresight to prepare for this. When the power went out in Idaho, the pump to their well stopped working. It was only ever a minor inconvenience though. They lived right by the river. You couldn't throw a stone without hitting water.

Her eyes drifted to the kitchen window, scanning the desert landscape of the dry valley that stretched below them. She knew she should try to make friends with the neighbors down there if they were going to be without power for a few weeks, but her first real encounter with anyone in the subdivision hadn't gone so well yesterday.

She glanced over to the hedges that partially blocked the view of the only other house up on the hill. *That's just great, Tessa.* The realization made her sick. *You panicked and now the old couple across the street are going to die of dehydration.* Were they smart enough to fill up some buckets? She really, really hoped so. They should have gone to the shelter anyway. What if something happened and they couldn't call for help? *You had to do what was right for your kids.* She tried to ease her own guilt but it wasn't working.

"Mom." Mason stood beside her as he waited to put his plate and cup in the sink.

"Sorry." She stepped back, staring at the dry faucet. "Emily, last bite. Then the two of you go get dressed."

Emily bounced up from her seat, dropping a piece of bacon on the floor that Moose licked up with a single tongue swipe. "But what about the chain?"

The staples ripped through the green construction paper circle as Tessa pulled it apart. Two pieces left, one blue and one yellow. Only one more chain to break. She let it go and it fluttered to the floor. Emily and Mason both dove for the strip, but Emily caught it this time.

She held the paper in the air triumphantly. "Two more days!"

And two days was too long to go without water. Three of them and you'd be dead. Tessa pulled her hair up into a messy bun and secured it with the elastic from her wrist. She really didn't want to do this, but it was the right thing to do. "Alright guys, get your shoes on. We're going to meet the neighbors."

"But we already know the neighbors." Mason hopped on one foot as he pulled his sneaker onto the other.

"How do you know them?" Tessa was trying to show Emily how to tie her laces again.

"Me and Dad met them. I thought you did too. They're just this old couple. But Arthur is a retired Marine and his wife Sally gave us popsicles."

Arthur? Tessa frowned. She definitely hadn't remembered his name or ever meeting them in person. It's not like she was anti-social or anything, but she hadn't really met anyone since they moved here. Between the kids and the dog and settling into the new house right before Landon left, she couldn't find the time. She knew she should have made some friends and formed some sort of support system before he deployed. But she didn't and now she could count on one hand the number of times she'd had a face to face conversation with another adult in the last six months. If she would have reached out, would that have made things easier? *Maybe you wouldn't have sent that email.*

Tessa cringed at the thought of the last words she'd sent to Landon and wished she could take them back. A moment of weakness and now she couldn't even get in touch with him, or anyone else for that matter. Nothing like getting social media taken away to make a person realize how truly alone they were.

"We'll be right back," Tessa assured Moose as he glanced over his shoulder. He gave a small *humph* and settled himself onto the couch to wait.

"Not too fast," Tessa called out when the kids raced ahead of her. She tried to think of what to say as she walked across the street. Sorry I took all our water wasn't the best introduction. But she reminded herself that she wasn't going there to make friends. The right thing to do was to offer a bucket or two if they weren't prepared. *Even though her kids might need it and the cops were just here offering assistance.* She almost turned back, putting an end to this stupid plan, but Mason skipped around the hedges dragging Emily by her hand and she had no choice but to follow them.

The driveway was lined with clay pots painted blue and red containing succulent plants with their fat green leaves that thrived in the desert soil. A wind chime hanging from the porch railing sang in the slight breeze, sending eerie notes along with the dust that blew across the yard. She'd never been close enough to their house before to see the two wooden rocking chairs that sat there hidden from view by the hedges. The garage door was open, the interior packed to the ceiling with shelves of organized bins, and the hood of the Dodge Ram sat propped open in front of it.

Tessa reached out to pull her kids back and remind them to behave, but the words got stuck in her throat when Arthur slammed the hood of the truck closed. The man's hair was gray beneath the fading USMC ball cap. His skin was wrinkled with age and his belly stretched out his stained white t-shirt, but his forearms were massive with veins bulging against the skin. He was much bigger in person than from across the street and stared at her with such intensity that she worried he already knew about the water and was about to demand an explanation. She forced herself to give a neighborly smile.

"Sorry to intrude," the words rushed from her lips. "I just wanted to make sure you guys were okay." Arthur grabbed a rag and rubbed it against his fingers, paying close attention to his wedding band which he twisted around twice. The action made Tessa pause. It was so much like Landon's nervous habit with his ring. "Do you have water? Do you need any? I filled up some buckets last night." She left out just how much. *No use in telling them you're crazy.*

Arthur grunted, turning away, and she took that as her clue to leave. "Come on kids." The screen door to the porch swung open and a fragile woman in a pale pink house dress hunched over her cane as she stepped outside.

"Good morning," Sally called out breathlessly. A smile lit up her light blue eyes. "Mason and Emily, right?"

Emily nodded, pulling her brother closer to the house. "Did your car get sick too? Mommy's car got sick, but Daddy's truck didn't and his ship can't get sick either. He's coming home in two days." Tessa resisted the urge to clamp her hand over her daughter's mouth and drag her away.

Sally laughed. "We saw you driving it yesterday and didn't know if your dad was home already. That thing sure makes a lot of noise. Mr. Arthur is fixing our truck up now and maybe he can take a look at your mom's car next." She motioned for the kids to come closer to the porch. "I made some fudge this morning, but I think I made too much. Would the two of you like to take some of it back home?" Sally glanced at Tessa with an eyebrow raised, the universal mom question hanging in the air.

"That's fine." Tessa sighed, feeling even more guilt. "About the water, I don't know if your pipes are tapped out too. I filled some buckets and can bring one over. I didn't think about both of us being up here on the hill during a power outage and I'm sorry for that."

"How many buckets did you fill?" Arthur tossed the rag onto the workbench in the garage and reached down to pull a pan out from under the truck.

"A few." She chewed the inside of her cheek, thinking about how truly ridiculous her panic must have been. No wonder the water stopped flowing after all she'd stored.

"Hush now." Sally waved her hand dismissively in the air as she stepped through the door. "We have plenty of water. Never thought the tap water tasted right here anyway. Let me go get you your fudge." A lizard shimmied across the porch and the kids dropped on their bellies to see where it was going next, leaving Tessa standing there alone with Arthur in the driveway.

She hugged her arms over her chest and tried to make small talk. "Did you figure out what's wrong with your truck?"

"Nothing's wrong with it. It just needed an oil change." He screwed the cap on the drip pan.

"Oh. I thought maybe it had the same issue as my Kia. There's a bunch of other cars that broke down on the streets too. I wasn't sure what happened." She shook her head, trying to clear the image from the gruesome car accident from her mind.

"Did you turn it on right after the power went out?" Arthur asked.

"Yeah. I had to go get Mason from school."

"You probably got zapped at just the right moment then."

"Zapped by what? The sun?" She glanced up at the burning ball of fire in the sky and eyed it warily.

"Energetic particles I would think," he said. "You've got the charge from the solar radiation mixing with local conductivity. We're on a hot bed of igneous rock here in Southern California. Couple that with the dry desert air and it's the perfect environment for massive static energy. You should have given it a few hours for the charge in the troposphere to return to normal before you fired up a multi-circuited device."

Tessa snapped her jaw shut. "I'm not going to pretend I understand half of what you're saying, but why did Landon's truck work fine?"

"Less computerized components? Less conductors to turn into inductors I assume." Arthur shrugged.

"Hang on." She took a step back. "How do you know all this? I thought you were a retired Marine."

"Are you saying Marines can't be smart?"

"I'm just saying I've got some extra packs of crayons laying around if you're hungry." Tessa cringed. *Why did I just say that?* Six months with minimal adult contact and she was already making awful jokes. The silence hung in the air between them. She really wanted to leave.

"Only if they're the red ones." He tried to keep a serious face, but the laughter in his eyes gave him away and she sighed in relief.

"So, you still think Landon is coming home in a few days then?" The question, and the way he phrased it, caught her off guard, lowering her defenses, and unwanted tears filled her eyes.

She blinked them away and tried not to give into the fear that was pushing at the edge of her sanity. "That was the plan as of yesterday."

"When was the last time you talked with him?" Arthur pulled off his cap and ran his hand through his hair. He was exactly the kind of man Landon would have made friends with. A tough old vet who asked pointed questions. She didn't like where this was going.

"He told me he was leaving Hawaii a few days ago." She left out the rest of the details. The message she'd sent after reading his email. The thought crossed her mind that maybe Landon did read it and chose not to respond. *Does he hate me now?* She hated herself for what she'd said.

"Hey now." Arthur looked away and she wiped her eyes, embarrassed for being so outwardly emotional in front of a complete stranger. "I'm sure he's alright and on his way back home. Those ships are floating faraday cages."

"Faraday what?" She tried to change the conversation.

"It's hard to explain." Arthur sighed. He glanced from her to the kids, his jaw working as if he was having some internal dilemma. It made the whole situation even more awkward. The screen door creaking on its hinges was a welcome sound. Emily and Mason jumped out of the way to give Sally room with their eyes glued to the wax paper wrapped square she held in her hands. The kids thanked her in unison as she handed the package to Mason and he turned his gap-toothed smile toward Tessa.

"You kids are sweet." Sally pat Emily on her head. "Be good for your mom."

"We will," Emily beamed and skipped away.

"Thanks for this." Tessa wrapped her arms over the kids' shoulders as they turned to leave. "And if you ever need water, let me know. I think I'm going to make some jerky this afternoon so the meat in the deep freezer doesn't go to waste if they can't get the power back on in the next few days. If you want some of that, I can bring it over in exchange for the fudge."

"Don't you dare think you owe us. That fudge is a gift." Sally wagged her finger and smiled. "Hey, I have an idea. Why don't you bring the kids over for Sunday dinner tomorrow? I need to clean out what's left in the fridge and we can have a real feast. Feel free to bring anything you want to get rid of."

"Sally," Arthur spoke her name as a warning before Tessa could turn down the invitation.

"Can it, Art." She glared at her husband and the big man seemed to shrink inside himself. Sally returned her attention to Tessa, her eyes sparkling with a youthful mischief. "There's a whole box of popsicles in the freezer. It'd be a shame if they went to waste."

"Can we, Mom?" Mason begged as he tugged on her arm.

"Please," Emily echoed.

"Thanks for the invitation, but we've got some chores to do." Tessa glanced at Arthur, but he was busying himself with opening the hood of the truck again.

"But Mom," Mason whined.

"Enough," she whispered just loud enough for him to hear.

Sally opened the screen door and waved them off. "Well, if you finish early, come on over."

Tessa glanced back over her shoulder as she guided her kids down the driveway. The hairs on the back of her neck were raised like someone was watching them. *Awesome. Now you're paranoid too.*

5

Tessa

Smoke from the grill drifted through the backyard while the kids rode their bikes around in the dirt. The smell of cooking meat had already permeated her clothes and hair. Tessa raised the lid and rotated the racks, trying to give it some air and keep the temperature at 150 degrees Fahrenheit. What she thought would take four hours was turning into six and would probably take eight to get all the moisture from the meat, but she wanted it as dry as possible so it would last for months if they ended up using it for snacks when the power came back on.

Pork loin and top round slices ¼ inch thick and soaked in a soy sauce marinade for a few hours sat curling at the edges on the grates. She couldn't bring herself to use the good steaks for this, the T-bones and ribeyes she'd gotten for her husband's homecoming. Those were still frozen so she moved them to the expensive Yeti cooler that Landon had to buy and they rarely ever used. If it didn't keep food cold for two weeks like he'd promised, then he could deal with the rotten meat when he got back. *If he got back.*

She pushed the thought away. Arthur was hinting at what she already knew could be possible, but she wasn't going to think along those lines right now. First things first, save whatever food she could

66

before it all turned bad and then deal with whatever was coming next.

On the stovetop, she made a skillet of ground beef and defrosting vegetables covered with cheese for dinner that the kids were probably going to complain about. There was pasta in the pantry which she knew they'd eat with it, but she wanted to save the dried goods for a while *just in case*. Mason was still upset that she'd said they weren't going to the neighbors for dinner tomorrow night so she was sure there would be little fights about everything. She glanced through the kitchen window at Sally and Arthur's house.

They seemed decent enough, but something was off. Especially with Arthur. It was like he was annoyed she existed, or confused about what to do with her. She couldn't put her finger on it, but she felt the same way about him and didn't want to get too close. Tessa tasted the concoction on the stove and added more dried basil.

Sally was adorable though. The way she handled Arthur made Tessa smile. She could just imagine them as a young couple with Sally's pleated swing skirt swaying with purpose as she marched around each new house at each duty station directing Arthur on where to hang the framed pictures. Maybe they'd been together all their lives. She hadn't asked enough questions. Did they have kids too?

Tessa turned off the gas on the stove and stared at the pan. There was definitely going to be a fight tonight. But she knew how to win.

"This is gross." Emily was the first to break, dropping her spoon into the bowl with a dramatic pout.

"Since you haven't tried it, I don't believe you." Tessa swallowed her food and smiled. It wasn't half bad and they didn't normally mind green things, but this many green things in a bowl was bound to shake them up. It wasn't all green. Bits of yellow corn and orange squares of carrots poked through like wildflowers in a meadow. A really bumpy and greasy meadow flavored with garlic, onions, and herbs. Mason chewed despondently, not even bothering to argue. Somehow that hurt her worse than the whining.

"I don't want to eat it." Emily pushed her bowl away. Landon always said she got her stubbornness from Tessa, but she was dead sure this attitude was inherited from the girl's grandfather.

"Fine, don't eat it." Tessa pointed her spoon at Mason. "But don't expect to eat all the ice cream in the house with us after we finish dinner."

As a rule, she never bribed, but natural consequences were a thing and the way Mason's eyes lit up as he shoveled a spoonful into his mouth was more than enough to absolve any mom guilt she had about bending the rules a little.

"You can do it." Mason gave Emily a pat on her back. She swallowed bravely and nodded, testing the food with her tongue. Mason laughed and let out a loud burp which had him cracking up, clutching his side as he tried to catch his breath. When he finally got under control, he grabbed his empty bowl and turned to Tessa. "Is there any more left?"

Multiple bowls of "it wasn't that bad" and two full tubs of ice cream later, Emily fell asleep on the couch next to Moose under the soft glow of the camping lantern while Tessa laid on the floor building Legos with Mason.

"Time for bed." She opened a bag of baby wipes and tried to get out some of the marshmallow that was still stuck in Emily's hair without waking her. Then she wiped down both of their faces and carried Emily upstairs.

"Mom, can we talk?" Mason stood waiting in the hallway dressed in clean pajamas as Tessa closed the door to Emily's room.

"What is it?" she whispered, putting a finger over her lips and motioning for him to get into bed. She dimmed the lantern and put it on his nightstand as she crawled under his twin size comforter and tucked it around their legs. "Are you still mad that I said no to dinner tomorrow night?"

"A little." Mason snuggled against her and bunched the pillow under his head. "I don't know why we don't go to friend's houses anymore like we used to do in North Carolina."

Way to sucker punch me, kid. She knew the move had been rough on him with Landon leaving less than two months after they got there. It'd been tough for them all. How could she explain to her son that she was tired of trying to make new friends just to lose them three years later when she was the one who reassured him countless times he'd make more? But it was different than normal with Sally and Arthur and whatever else was happening now.

She didn't even want to admit to herself the growing fear that if the power didn't come back on and the stores stayed closed that food was going to be scarce in a few weeks. She'd already taken all the water. She couldn't take their food too. They were old, and if they weren't going to the shelter then she worried the longer this went on, and the closer they got, she'd be forced to take care of them. *It would already be hard enough without two more mouths to feed.*

"How about this?" Tessa rubbed circles into his back, soothing him to sleep like she did when he was younger. "When your dad gets home, we'll invite both of them over for dinner here. That way Dad will have a new friend too."

"But the popsicles are going to melt by then." Mason squeezed his eyes closed.

"That's what all this is about?" She pulled her hand away and stared at him. "Popsicles?" He buried his face in the pillow. Tessa laughed, kissing him on the head. "I can't even deal with you tonight. I love you. Go to sleep. We have a big day tomorrow."

A low growl pulled her from her dreams. Tessa groaned, pulling the quilt over her head, as she tried to cling to the fading image of Landon cornering her in the kitchen with his shirt soaked in sweat and lifting her onto the counter. His thumb was sliding up the curve of her neck, tilting her face to his, and she ran her hands over the taunt muscles of his back…

The furious clicks of claws against the tiled floor and a sharp bark forced her eyes to open. *Dang it, Moose.* Did she let him out to use the bathroom before bed? Moose's bark deepened, becoming a warning that someone was here. She searched around in the dark for her phone to check the time. The familiar weight of it in her hand was reassuring, until she touched the screen and pressed the power button. Reality brought her fully awake.

Someone knocked on the door sending Moose into a frenzy of barks that echoed through the house. She threw off the blankets and raced across the room. The soft moonlight shining through the window lit her way. *Maybe Landon is home early.* She stopped in the doorway, holding the frame with her hand. *Landon has a key.* Whoever it was, knocked again. She shook her head as she continued forward down the stairs. *It's probably just the neighbors. Maybe they need help.*

"Anyone there?" a strange man's voice called from outside the house. Moose paced in front of the door, barking aggressively with spit flying from his mouth. He never acted like that for strangers. Tessa turned and ran back up the stairs with her heart pounding in her chest. There was no way to call the cops. Was there anywhere to run? She could go to

Arthur and Sally's with the kids, but what would happen if they didn't answer the door?

Breathe. She fumbled in the dark closet through Landon's clothes, feeling for the wool shirt. Her fingers slipped into the breast pocket and she pulled out the key to the gun safe.

The man knocked again and Moose's barking grew in intensity until it reverberated in her skull. *I hear you, buddy.* The light from the moon shone on the metallic pink case on the top shelf of the gun safe. And in it was the stupid pink and black SCCY CPX-2 9mm Landon had given her as a Christmas present three years ago when he thought he was being cute. The .30-30 might invoke more fear, but she'd never shot it so she left it against the rest as she yanked out the joke of a semi-automatic pistol.

"Hey! I know someone's in there."

Moose let loose a feral growl before resuming his frantic barks. Tessa rushed down the stairs, pushing the magazine in the wrong way and slipping on the third step. She caught herself against the banister and turned the magazine around so it slid into place.

"Mom?" His sleepy voice called from above her as she reached the bottom step. Mason rubbed his eyes, trying to see through the darkness.

"Go to your sister's room and lock the door. Don't come out until I say it's okay." Somehow, she managed to keep her voice even and steady. A command he wouldn't argue with. His silhouette disappeared as he ran to Emily's room. She had to breathe, to will her heart to slow down. Moose's barking was making her panic. *Maybe it's just the police.*

"Open up!" A fist beat against her door.

Tessa crouched low as she made her way across the living room to where Moose was pacing. "Down," she commanded and the dog obeyed, falling to the floor with a heavy sigh now that his job was done. Flashlight beams shone through the paneled glass and she scooted to the side, pressing herself against the wall and the front door so the light wouldn't touch her.

"Just smash it in, William. No one's home."

"Will you shut up and let me think? There's a big dog in there."

"You have a bat. Kill the dog. What's the problem here?"

The flashlight beam reflected off Moose's big brown eyes as he cocked his head to the side. Tessa motioned for him to stay down, clutching the pistol in her hand as she risked a peek over the edge of the glass panel that lined the door.

Two men stood on her porch, shifting anxiously as they looked over their shoulders and both of them holding flashlights. The bigger man with the bat stood further back. *William,* she assumed. The second reached up to knock again. She ducked back down and pressed the pistol to her thigh to make her hand stop shaking.

"Please," the second man cried. "We need help out here."

"Good one." William chuckled. "That'll get their attention."

Tessa held her hand over her mouth to muffle the sound of her silent scream. If she opened the door, would they overpower her? She could shoot through the glass, but what if there were more of them outside and then they would know she was in here. Their nervous laughter filled the quiet house. They were coming in one way or the other. She had to act.

She slid along the wall until she reached the kitchen. Her bare feet left quiet footsteps as she raced across the tiles. Moose leapt up to follow her and she stopped him with one word, "Mason." He grunted in understanding and turned to flee upstairs. She couldn't let herself think about what would happen to her kids if she got hurt, couldn't give into the soul crushing fear of what might happen if these creeps got inside. She just had to get them away from her house. She had to get them away from her kids.

The back door slammed too loud behind her and she took off running to the fence, praying they didn't hear anything. The moon was so brilliant it lit up the desert ground like freshly fallen snow. She kept herself pressed against the side of the house and scanned the road for a car or more people. Nothing else moved in the night.

Silently, she broke away from the cover of the stucco siding and slipped into the concave of the closed garage door. Her pulse was so loud it rang in her ears and she held her breath waiting for them to hear her.

"Alright. It's sketch standing here like this. Open the door already."

Tessa looked around the garage door frame to the walkway that led to her front stoop. She was hidden in the shadows, but the moon illuminated their pock marked faces and the tweaker sores distorting their skin with purplish bruises. It was just the two men and a baseball bat. She took a steadying breath. *Only two men and a bat and a stupid pink gun.*

"Get off my property." The men turned at the sound of her voice. She raised the gun and held it steady. "Go now. I'm not playing."

"Hey, it's okay sweet pea." William smiled with rotting gums. "Don't be scared of us. We just need some help. The ATMs aren't working and the shelters can't feed everyone, you know. We were hoping you might have some food or money to spare."

"I didn't stutter." She didn't want to talk. She wanted them to leave. William took advantage of the shadow cast on the walkway by the cloud passing over the moon to lunge forward with the bat.

She fired. But the instant she did, she saw her mistake. The recoil had thrown her aim off and the bullet whizzed by his shoulder into the side of the house. The half second of panic was eased by the memory of Landon's voice in her ear at the shooting range, *"again."* She repositioned her aim with her finger on the trigger just as William crumpled to the ground.

"What the hell, man? You shot him!" the second tweaker screamed as he jumped off her doorstep, trampling her flower garden when he took off running for the desert hill. *Did I shoot him?* It all happened so fast she didn't have time to think.

The baseball bat rolled down the walkway and she reached to pick it up with the 9mm trained on William's head. Dark liquid oozed onto the concrete. She used the bat to turn him over. William's right ear was a bloodied mess with the bullet lodged somewhere in his brain. *Did it ricochet off something?* She stared in confusion at the mess of a human who was rotting long before his death.

The heavy crack of a gunshot snapped her from her trance and she ducked, pressing herself against the side of the house.

"Got 'em," Arthur's voice echoed through the night as he stood from the cover of the hedges and walked out onto the moonlit road. He lowered his rifle and let it hang from the sling around his shoulder.

"Did you do this?" Tessa looked to the burly old neighbor as he walked up her driveway and back to the body that was staining her yard.

"Yeah." Arthur pulled off his ballcap and rubbed his eyes with his arm. "I couldn't get a clear shot with them in the doorway like that. Thanks for drawing them out."

Some rational part of her brain knew she should thank him, but nothing was rational anymore and adrenaline snaked its way through her body setting her blood on fire. "I didn't need your help. I could have handled them on my own."

He glanced down at the pink and black 9mm held in her hands. Warmth spread to her face as she tucked the pistol into the waistband of her pajama shorts. She avoided his curious gaze and crouched down to get a good grip on William's ankles while the smell of his unwashed body accosted her nose.

"What are you doing?" Arthur asked.

"Getting him off my yard and out of sight so the kids don't see this mess." She groaned under the dead man's weight as she dragged him down the driveway.

"Let me help." Arthur moved the sling so his rifle was on his back.

Tessa's shoulders tensed and she clenched her teeth. "I said I don't need any help."

Arthur stood in the middle of the road watching as she pulled the body across the asphalt to the empty lot of sagebrush on the side of the hill. Goat heads tore into the bare flesh of her feet, but she didn't stop moving until she couldn't see her house anymore. She dropped his ankles and picked out the thorns from her skin, barely feeling the sting. *This is so wrong on so many levels.*

She couldn't look at the dead tweaker anymore, but she couldn't just leave him there like that. This felt like a bad science fiction movie. She knew she should call the cops and report everything. *Except, I don't have a phone!* The anger came in waves. None of this was right. She killed a man—*no, Arthur killed him*— and someone needed to be notified. He should be in jail, not dead. But this stupid druggie came to her home and threatened to kill her dog. What if he'd actually gotten in? What would he have done to her kids?

And what happens when the cops find out you didn't report a crime? She yanked her hair into a messy bun, trying hard to focus on the facts and not the fear fueled rage that was tearing her apart. *You're an accomplice to this murder.* Was it murder? She didn't know. Tomorrow, she needed to drive down to the police station and report it. But what would happen if they accused her of something and tossed her into jail? The kids needed her to be there for them. And what would happen if they took her truck? Officer O'Brien seemed pretty keen on knowing what vehicles still worked. She kicked the nasty body with her bare foot, cursing the druggie who put her in this position.

But she didn't shoot him. *Arthur shot him.* That was the truth and she could always explain it was self-defense if her name got pulled into this mess. *What would Landon say?* He of all people would understand. She drew in a ragged breath, still full of adrenaline fumes and rage. This wasn't her problem. She had enough problems of her own. Tessa marched up the hill.

Arthur was still standing there with his arms folded across his chest. *He's the one who pulled the trigger so it's his duty to report it.* Now that she had settled it, and made a firm decision, she nodded once in his direction as she stormed up her driveway.

His soft chuckle danced through the night as he turned to leave. "You make sure you bring those kids over tomorrow. Dinner is at 5 o'clock."

She wasted half a bottle of bleach and a gallon of water scrubbing the blood from the walkway. Whatever stains remained she hoped wouldn't be too visible in the light of day. She wasn't trying to wipe away the evidence, she was trying to make sure her kids didn't see. And her knuckles bleeding from hitting them against the concrete with the sponge was atonement for whatever sin she'd committed in protecting her home.

The whole situation had lasted no more than twenty minutes, but she felt like she'd aged ten years. Her body ached from the tension and exertion as she put the cleaning supplies away. Moose's growl was no more than a low whimper when she stepped onto the bottom of the stairs.

"It's alright." The rapid thump of his tail hit the carpeted floor, but he didn't move away from Emily's closed door until she'd reached the top step.

He yawned, stretching out his back and padded into her room. Tessa cracked open Emily's door.

Mason had fallen asleep on the floor using the giant teddy bear as a pillow and Emily was buried deep in her bed under a mountain of stuffed toys. The weight of everything that happened tonight crashed down at once as she stared at her babies who'd slept through gunshots outside of their home. Tessa didn't want to leave them alone. She wanted them safely tucked into her bed, but she couldn't stop shaking and the tears fell fast as a painful knot tightened in her chest.

She backed away from the room, unloading the magazine and clearing the pistol before she stowed it in her bedside table. Sobs racked her body as she climbed onto the bed. *I almost killed a man tonight.* The adrenaline that fueled her earlier ebbed away, leaving her hollow and weak and alone. She pulled her knees to her chest and hugged herself as tears ran down her face. *Is this what the world is like without power? Vigilante justice and no one to call for help?*

Her father's warning raced through her mind as she rocked back and forth. She should take the kids to base where it might be safer. *But what if Landon never comes back?* The fear was too much. She squeezed her eyes shut and tried to wish it all away. The mattress creaked under Moose's weight.

"You're not supposed to be up here," she whispered. He circled around the foot of the bed and settled onto the quilt beside her. She ran her fingers through his thick brown fur and buried her face against it, listening to his snores and trying not to focus too long on any one thought until the rays of the dangerous sun crept over the mountains to start a new day.

6
Landon

GySgt. Fuimaono's large frame filled the open hatch to the berthing. A crooked smile lit up his face as his eyes danced around the room. "Field day, gentleman. Up and at it. And you better not bring the head mop in here again or I'm making you all lick the floors." Sgt. Sierra groaned as he slid down from his rack. His feet hit the deck next to Landon's boots.

"You've got to be kidding me. We just did this two days ago," he mumbled under his breath. Landon nodded, smoothing the corners of his sheets into 45-degree angles on the thin mattress pad.

Sgt. Sierra stretched his neck from side to side, popping the bones down his spine, and turned to the others with a motivated clap. "You heard him, boys. Let's get moving."

The complaints were minimal as the Marines and sailors scrubbed every nook and cranny of the ship. Yesterday was spent in general quarters and there was only so much down time a person could take. Everyone was bored enough to be grateful for something to do.

But the menial work wasn't hard enough to quiet Landon's mind. His thoughts raced as he swept the deck and his jaw hurt from clenching his teeth.

The rumors had spread like wildfire. Supposedly a solar event of this magnitude could wipe out the power grid. Some guy heard from someone who worked in IT that this kind of thing could also fry every electronic device that had a computer chip in it. Then Cpl. Matthews argued that their phones still worked and that the IT was an idiot. Sgt. Ballis stepped in and explained that was an EMP that would take out handheld devices but a solar storm couldn't damage much. And someone else pointed out that the ships NAV was down and so it apparently did something.

Landon pulled his phone from his pocket and turned on. Still no service, but he never got any inside of the ship and the CO wasn't letting anyone above deck so he couldn't check to see if he could get any bars outside. That was another rumored issue, the ship's medical SMO supposedly said something about potentially dangerous UV rays.

But the worst was not knowing anything for certain. It was all just rumors. There was no further trickle down of information from the higher-ups. No communication with the outside world. Nothing but hours spent in your own head sweeping dust bunnies out from under the racks.

"Hey Doc. You okay?" Sgt. Sierra came over with a bottle of cleaning solution in one hand and a rag thrown over his shoulder.

"Yeah." Landon reached for the dustpan. "You?"

"Not really." Sgt. Sierra scratched his fingers through the black stubble of his high and tight fade. When they were younger, he wore it longer. But there wasn't much left to it now. "I can't stop thinking about what this all could mean. Do you remember the rolling blackouts in Syria? You think it's going to be like that?"

"Syria was a worn zone," Landon pointed out. "This is America were talking about. But all we are getting is rumors. Just let it go until we find out the truth."

"But come on. What if we're coming home to a third world country or something with all the power out?" Sgt. Sierra lowered his voice so the others wouldn't hear. "What if it turns into Mexico?"

"Dude, you're Mexican." Landon shook his head. "Don't say racist stuff like that."

"It's not racist," Sgt. Sierra protested. "And I'm Mexican-American, but my abuela told me all about how she lived in a mud hut with no power. I keep thinking if that's what we're coming back to, how the hell are they going to survive? Americans don't know what it's like out there."

"You just said you were American." Landon sighed.

"You know exactly what I mean, Doc." Sgt. Sierra gave him the same pointed look he'd given so many times. They'd been deployed together when he was a Lance Corporal and Landon was an HN. Two scared kids with no clue what was going on. Not much had changed since then, minus the haircut and the responsibility that comes with not being able to tell anyone you're scared.

"Hey Sierra," Landon clapped him on the back, causing him to drop the cleaning solution bottle, "do me a favor and shut up."

Sgt. Sierra smiled and then sucker punched him in the arm before he walked away. "Good talk. Want to hit the gym later?"

Landon moved forward to fill the empty space at the head of the line when a spot finally opened up inside the gym. Sgt. Sierra leaned against the bulkhead beside him, muttering under his breath about "motards" as he plugged his headphones in. The line ran down the passageway and more than a few guys climbed down the ladder well over the past hour and groaned as they saw the wait before climbing back up again. The other night was a miracle with an empty gym. Now everyone and their mother wanted to blow off some steam.

Landon scrolled through his playlist. His thumb hovered above one of Tessa's favorite songs. Their wedding wasn't anything special, just a few friends at the local courthouse, but the week that followed they'd toured Yellowstone and camped under the stars. He pressed play and the folk notes drifted through his earbuds, reminding him of those precious carefree days where she turned the radio up and sang offkey with her bare feet on the dashboard and the wind from the open window blowing hair around her face. He closed his eyes, getting lost in the memory. *God, I can't wait to go home.*

"Doc, we might have a problem." Sgt. Sierra ripped his headphones out as he elbowed Landon's stomach and pointed inside the gym.

A beefed-up dude with rope like veins and thick neck was knife handing someone seated on the lat pull-down machine.

"I've got fifty bucks that says it's that kid again." Sgt. Sierra chuckled. Landon tried to glance around the meat-eater's back but he couldn't get a visual on the guy's target. No one in the gym moved from their equipment, but a few of them cast amused glances at the scene. Landon sighed as he walked through the hatch.

"What's going on?" He sidestepped the big guy to see the Boatswain's Mate who always carried around drumsticks in the back of his shorts seated on the plastic seat. His cheeks were flushed, but he wasn't moving.

Spit flew from meat-eater's mouth as he thrust his knife hand toward the kid. "Forty reps of three pull-downs with 5lb weights. He's been doing this for over an hour. You're done, son. Get the hell out of here and let someone else use the machine."

"Yeah, I can see how that might be frustrating." Landon rubbed the back of his neck. "Maybe let him have a final set. What do you say, squid? One last round and then try something else?"

"I think this jerk shouldn't worry about what I'm doing and maybe he should be the one laying off the weights. He's already bursting at the seams. If anyone is done in here, it's him."

Oh. So you have a death wish. Landon groaned as he caught the full force of meat-eater's fist in the palm of his hand and twisted it back, immobilizing him by the arm. He didn't notice Sierra was behind him until he grabbed the big guy's other shoulder.

"I'm going to get him out of here." Landon motioned to the kid.

Sgt. Sierra nodded, tightening his grip on meat-eater. "You're going to calm down before you get written up." The fight drained from the big guy and he lowered his head, suddenly very aware of the seriousness of what he almost did.

"Come on." Landon tugged the young sailor off of the machine. His face was pale and he glanced nervously over his shoulder like he couldn't believe he'd said that. *You and me both, kid.* He guided him outside the gym and toward the ladder well while the sailor stared at his feet.

"Listen, we're all on edge here." Landon's frustration eased as he assumed the role of parent lecturing a child. "But picking fights isn't going to do anyone any good."

"He started it…" the sailor began.

"And I'm finishing it," Landon cut him off. "On that note, since you want to act like you're five, when you see a line of people outside the gym, don't waste everyone's time by hogging a single machine for an hour. If I find out you do something like that again, I'm getting your LPO involved. Do you understand me?"

"Yes HM2." The sailor refused to look him in the eye.

"Alright then, get out of here." Landon stood with his arms crossed as the kid scrambled up the ladder well. This game was making him tired. He was sick of taking care of grown men and women who should have had a shred of common sense somewhere in their thick skulls. They weren't all that bad, but sometimes…

Landon shook his head. If he was supposed to be a babysitter, he'd rather be at home with his own kids. The responsibility of this job would only get harder the longer he stayed in. Not reenlisting was looking better every day. Ten years had already been too long. Would Mason be stupid and reckless like this when he turned eighteen? He seriously hoped not. Now Emily on the other hand got the same stubbornness and temper as her mother. She was bound to raise hell growing up just like Tessa did. *Whatever is happening back home, Tessa is strong enough to handle it.* He smiled to himself as he thought of his red-headed girls and went back to the gym to outrun his home sickness on the treadmill.

7

The yellow strip of paper tearing beneath her fingers gave renewed hope for the day. She tossed it to the side, not bothering to see who caught it, and focused on the remaining blue circle. *One more day.* After tomorrow she'd decide what to do and hopefully, she wouldn't have to make that decision alone. But for today, she was going to believe everything would be okay.

"I don't have to go to school tomorrow, right?" Mason asked as she climbed down from the chair and carried it back to the kitchen table. Her heart skipped a beat. *Would they still have school with no power?* "You said I could come with you to pick up Dad."

"Yep. No school tomorrow." *And maybe not for a long time.* The hope of a good day was starting to slip, but she forced herself to smile.

"Can we play Barbies?" Emily dumped out the bucket of half clothed plastic dolls onto the rug.

"Not right now." Tessa grabbed the roll of paper towels off the counter. "You guys know what today is. Go start cleaning your rooms."

Sunlight filled the garage as she pushed open the metal door. The sky was brilliant blue and cloudless, another perfect Southern California spring day. It made the events of last night seem like a bad dream. But she scanned the road anyway and put the loaded pistol on the shelf within easy reach *just in case*. Her gaze drifted to the hill where she dragged the tweaker's body last night, a trail of dark red sat drying in the sun, and the inner turmoil threatened to consume her. She inhaled deeply, trying to focus on the task at hand instead. There'd be time to speak with Arthur later. Maybe she'd take the kids over for dinner after all, but first she had to get the house ready for tomorrow.

She went to the curb to pull the trash and recycling bins back to the house. Both of them were still full. The truck never came to pick them up yesterday. *They'll probably be here today.* She left them where they were and tried to shove the full garbage bag from the house on top of last week's waste. The cardboard boxes could be burned later.

In the garage, she dug through the workbench drawers looking for the cordless handheld shop vacuum to try and get Moose's hair off the couch. Landon had too many tools and he didn't use half of them, but this one could come in handy now. *And, of course, the battery is dead.* She put it back and kicked the drawer closed. At least the broom still worked.

She pulled out the camping bin they hadn't used in over a year, hoping to find extra batteries for the flashlights. The sun tan lotion bottle that was in there had exploded coating everything in a pasty white grime mixed with dirt. She also couldn't find any batteries, but at least she had a rag nearby to give the outdoor cooking utensils a quick wipe down.

Today is a good day. She tried to shove the bin back into place on the shelf above her head, but something must have shifted when she pulled it out. She dropped the bin and climbed the shelves to see what was going wrong now. There was a stack of boxes lining the back of the shelf behind where the bin usually sat and one had tipped over. She tugged it forward, balancing with her toes on the ledge below and clinging to the rack with one arm. It was too heavy to lift with one hand but she managed to push it upright. *Meal, Ready to Eat* was printed on the side.

Tessa left it there, smiling as she jumped to the ground. She didn't know that Landon had stored cases of MREs and couldn't wait to kiss him for being the pack rat that he was. *Today is a very good day.*

"It's clean, Mom." Mason fell face first onto her bed.

"Are you sure about that?" Tessa leaned against the broom handle, feeling ridiculous for sweeping the carpet but there was dog hair everywhere and she had to at least try to do something about it.

"Let me check." He groaned as he rolled off the bed and marched with his shoulders hunched right back to his room. Tessa shook her head. *Seven going on seventeen.* He needed more time with his dad.

Emily's room was worse than when she'd started. They all pitched in to get it done. The morning had a slight breeze and she'd opened all the windows, but by late afternoon she walked around closing and locking all of them as the sun decided to change the temperature of the earth.

"Can we go play outside?" Mason helped put away the last of the cleaning supplies.

"For a little bit, but don't get too dirty," Tessa said. "We're going out for dinner." Mason cheered, pumping his fist in the air as he raced outside to tell Emily the good news.

The cherry pie in its cardboard box was still cold even as it sat defrosting in the deep freezer. Tessa pulled it out and moved the last of the yogurt and cheese from the fridge to put in its empty space. The fridge was useless now after three days with no power. Everything she hadn't yet used had been transferred to the deep freezer. *And we're almost out of milk.* At least Emily wasn't drinking three cups of it a day anymore and needing one to fall asleep. *I wonder if anyone is selling a cow.*

"Come on. Let's go." Mason checked the time on Tessa's phone that she'd let charge in the truck while they were cleaning. The whole device wasn't useful for anything other than a clock at the moment and time was starting to not matter much anymore.

"Wait for me." Tessa grabbed her keys and made sure to lock the door this time. Moose stared at her expectantly, his tail wagging from side to side.

"Sorry, bud. You stay here and watch the house for me."

Sally wore a blue dress patterned with sunflowers that brought out the color of her eyes and she'd teased her hair just enough to frame her delicate face. She even had pink lipstick on. Tessa glanced down at her jeans and then looked to her dirty children as they raced inside the house, praying they didn't smell too bad. *Real baths for everyone tomorrow.*

"Thank you for inviting us." The waterlogged cardboard crushed under her fingers as she gripped the pie box in her hands.

"I'm glad you came. Us military wives need to stick together." A smile lit up Sally's face and she wrapped one arm around Tessa's waist while keeping her weight on the cane. Despite the fragility of the hug, it was full of warmth. She hadn't been hugged by anyone other than her kids in six months. It felt nice.

Steam filled the kitchen making the air hot and humid. Tessa walked to the counter to drop off the pie and glanced into the oversized pot on the stove. Water boiled gently against glass mason jars and lids.

"Are you canning something?"

"The real question is what am I not canning." Sally laughed. The melodic sound filled Tessa with unexpected peace. "Let me turn this off for now and we'll get the table set. Kids, can you come get these plates?"

Mason and Emily skipped into the kitchen and waited for instructions. It always amazed Tessa that no matter how they behaved at home, with guests they were nothing but polite. She smiled then, a little proud that maybe some of what she was teaching had stuck.

"How long have you and Arthur been married?" she asked to start the small talk.

Sally smiled with a faraway look in her eyes as she handed Tessa another water bottle. "Since he was seventeen and I was sixteen. It'll be fifty years next March. You should have seen how much my parents hated him after he enlisted and we eloped."

"That's basically our story too," Tessa said. "Except we were both nineteen. Landon had joined the Navy and I was in college. I wasn't sure that the long-distance thing was going to last. But he came home on leave to visit and fate had other plans." She looked over at Mason who stood waiting for the silverware.

Sally cast a knowing look between the two of them and then burst into laughter. "I bet your parents loved that."

Tessa couldn't help but smile at the memory that had plagued her entire adult life. "It's just my dad, actually. And he absolutely hated it."

"Oh, you poor girl." Sally wiped the happy tears from her eyes and bit her lip to hide her smile. "Does he still hate him?"

"He does," Tessa groaned. "Eight years later and he still blames Landon for me dropping out of college and leaving home."

"He'll get over it someday." Sally pat her on the arm. "It took my parents twenty years to warm up to Art. Trust me, you still have time."

Even though it was too hot in the kitchen and her kids were starting to argue in the dining room about where the silverware should be placed and the power still wasn't turned back on, she felt a comforting sort of peace in talking with someone who'd walked her path before. "Someday you'll have to tell me how you convinced them to accept Arthur's role in your life."

"What role?" The interior garage door slammed behind Arthur and Tessa jumped.

"Nothing dear." Sally leaned on her cane, standing on her toes to kiss his scruffy cheek. His rough stance melted against her tiny frame and Tessa lowered her eyes, embarrassed and filled with the familiar longing that made her hate romance movies when Landon was away.

"We were just chatting." Sally pointed to the dining room. "Now go wash up and help those kids with the forks. Dinner is almost ready."

The smell of Thanksgiving, smoked ham and roasted vegetables, wafted through the house when Sally opened the sliding glass door to the back porch.

"Can you grab those gloves and bring this in for me?" She motioned to the oven mittens hanging on the hook over the stove. Tessa slid them on and grabbed the pot off the grill.

"That's good." Sally nodded, inspecting the succulent feast. "Now let's start eating. Arthur gets grumpy when he's hungry."

The plastic water bottle crinkled in her hand as Emily sucked the rest of it down. She hadn't wanted any water all day, but she had to choose now to be thirsty.

"Let me grab you another one." Even with her cane, Sally was quick to her feet.

"She's fine." Tessa paused mid-bite. The small talk at dinner had made it too easy to forget why she was even here in the first place. *The water. The dead tweaker.* She shook her head. "I should have brought them drinks. Besides, if she has too much then she might wet the bed."

Emily's jaw dropped and the potatoes almost fell from her mouth. "You're lying. I don't pee the bed anymore. I'm a big girl now." She folded her small arms over her body, fuming at her mother. Tessa felt heat rush to her face.

"It's okay." Sally turned to the kitchen. "I told you we had more than enough." Arthur stared at her with his brow furrowed and Tessa lowered her eyes to avoid his gaze.

"So…" she began awkwardly. "Do you two have any children?" Even as she said it, she knew it was stupid to ask. There were no family pictures on the walls. They hadn't volunteered the information. To get out of one uncomfortable conversation, she'd dove headfirst into another. *Great.*

"One girl," Arthur said. "Anissa is in the Airforce. She's stationed in Germany right now."

Tessa sighed in relief. "You must be so proud."

"She's a good girl." Arthur's voice cracked as he spoke and his hand was shaking when he took another bite of ham.

"Are you alright?" she asked.

"He's fine." Sally reappeared with the water bottle and leaned against his side for support as she screwed off the lid. "We're just worried about how widespread this is and if she is doing alright or if she'll ever be able to make it home."

Tessa swallowed hard; the warm food suddenly cold in her stomach. "I'm sure it isn't like this everywhere and she'll make it home as soon as she can."

"We hope so too." Sally nodded as she handed Emily the water bottle. The girl took it with a sideways glance of triumph directed at her mother.

After everyone had cleared their plates, Mason and Emily offered to carry the dishes to the sink.

"You're raising good ones." Sally winked when Mason took her plate away.

Tessa rolled her eyes. "I'm raising devils who know how to put on halos when there are popsicles involved."

Arthur snorted and a grin lit up his face. "Then you're raising smart ones too."

"I hope so." Tessa smiled, glad he'd warmed up a bit after the quiet rest of dinner.

"I hear you want some popsicles." Sally pushed back her chair. Mason and Emily popped their heads around the doorframe to the kitchen and nodded.

"Alright you little devils." Sally laughed as she hobbled out of the room. "There's six left and you can have the whole box, but eat them outside on the porch so they don't drip all over the floor."

The kids thanked Sally over and over again as she went with them outside and closed the sliding glass door. Their excitement made Tessa happy, but her face fell when she turned to see Arthur staring at her again.

She twisted her hands together under the table. "About last night, I didn't mean to be rude to you. It all kind of caught me off guard and I couldn't believe that would happen up here. I know there is a huge problem with meth addicts in the area, but our hill always seemed so safe. Thank you for your help though. Did you go report the shooting to the police?"

"The police?" Arthur smirked. "Do you really think they're going to care after all they are dealing with now? That's two less tweakers they have to worry about. If you're feeling guilty, let it go. Things are going to get much worse very soon."

"Do you really think so?" She took her napkin and swept the crumbs from where Emily had sat into a neat pile on the oak table to give her hands something to do. With the way he was talking, she didn't want to make him upset and so she fed into the craziness. He'd killed two people last night like it was nothing. *Change of plans. You go to the cops after you pick up Landon tomorrow.*

"Unfortunately, I do." Arthur sighed as he leaned back in his chair. "But I don't think you are grasping the seriousness of what is happening right now. Those punks were opportunists. They weren't even hungry yet. In a few days when the food runs out, you're going to see what humans are truly capable of."

Tessa shook her head. "They've got shelters set up to provide for everyone in town. It's not like they'll just let them starve."

"You're not understanding this. Those shelters are filling up by the minute. Where are they going to get the food to feed everyone for the next few months? There's not a city in America that has enough food on hand to feed the population for more than three days. Most households don't have enough food to last two weeks. And I can guarantee there's even less that store enough water to last longer than a

99

week once the pipes run dry." Arthur paused and gave her a pointed look, waiting for this all to sink in. "But I'm curious to know why you didn't take the kids to the shelter. How much water do you have?"

"We didn't need the help." Tessa bit her lip. She knew that the water was an issue. "Like I said, if you need some water, I can share it. I wasn't thinking when I filled both the tubs and a few five-gallon buckets and all the jugs in the house." She was rambling but she couldn't stop, "I was worried about the kids and making sure we had enough. For some reason, I thought it might shut off with the power immediately but I didn't think about it being gravity fed and what that might mean for you. I'll stop in the subdivision tomorrow and see if their water is still flowing so we can fill up some extra buckets if you need it and don't want to take it from me."

Arthur stared above her head, mouthing silent numbers, before he returned his attention to her. "So, you have about twenty-eight days of water give or take, all depending on how you use it. How much food do you have?"

The question suddenly felt dangerous after everything he'd just said and Tessa froze, wide-eyed. He may be her neighbor, he may have helped her last night, but she didn't really know this man who was so flippant about killing people in her yard.

"Enough for my kids," she whispered as she stood from the chair.

"Sit down." Arthur folded his arms over his chest. "I'm not going to take your food. I'm just

100

trying to figure out if you're too prideful or too stupid to not go to the shelter."

"I'm sorry." Tessa took a step back. "Would that make you stupid too? Sure you can shoot, but what if you break a hip or something with no way to call an ambulance?"

"What did you say?" Arthur's deep chested laughter filled the room.

Her cheeks were bright red and she lowered her face. "I didn't mean it as an insult. I… I'm really worried about everything and if something happens to you or Sally, I don't know how I can help you when it's just me and the kids. When Landon comes home tomorrow, I think we should all get together and come up with a plan for how to get through the next few weeks or however long it takes to get the power back on."

His expression turned somber, the laughter dying like a snuffed flame. "Humor me for a second, how much food do you have?"

"Enough for three to four weeks." She didn't mention the cases of MREs she found in the garage. She was only humoring him after all. "Why do you need to know?"

"It's a start." He pushed himself away from the table. "And do you have something more than that frilly pink pistol?"

"Landon might…" Her voice trailed off. *Where is he going with this?*

Arthur nodded, hearing what she didn't say, and headed to the strange door bordered with mosaic tiles in the middle of the living room. "Come with me. I think it's time you learn exactly how real this is."

Tessa hesitated at the top stair as she held open the door. "You have a basement in Southern California?"

He grunted in response and walked into the darkness below. There was an audible click and an electric lantern cast an eerie glow on the steps, illuminating the dust particles as they flew around the stagnant air. She leaned back to look through the kitchen and the sliding glass door. Emily's chin was dyed blue from the popsicle and she was tucked beneath Sally's arm while Mason showed off his ninja skills to the two of them. She didn't want to tear them away from their fun, but when Arthur's deep voice called out, "Are you coming or not?" she almost ran.

If he was going to murder you, why would he help save you the other night? She inhaled deeply as she took the next step.

"Took you long enough," Arthur grumbled as he fidgeted with the dials of a device that looked like a police scanner on top of the folding card table under the lantern that hung from the ceiling. His back was turned to her so she took a quick look around the cellar. Metal shelves like the ones in his garage were packed to the top with plastic storage containers. The entire shelf at the back of the small room was filled with glass jars that reflected the light of the lantern. She took another step forward to better read the meticulously handwritten labels on the containers.

Gauze and tourniquets. Misc. medical supplies. Batteries. Water purification. Cold weather survival…

"Calling Whiskey-Alpha-6-Hotel-Bravo-Kilo, this is November-Alpha-6-Echo. I repeat…" Tessa jumped at the sound of Arthur's commanding voice as he spoke into the handset speaker and she backed away from the snooping position she'd wandered into.

"November-Alpha-6-Echo, this is Whiskey-Alpha-6-Hotel-Bravo-Kilo." The radio buzzed to life.

Arthur motioned for Tessa to come closer. "Are you ready for this?"

Every part of her being was screaming at her to run up the steps and drag her kids back to her house. This could wait until tomorrow. *Just give me one last good day where I'm not scared out of my wits and wondering what will happen next.* "Yes." She nodded.

"Alright," he whispered as he pressed his thumb against the button on the receiver and held it close to his mouth. "WA6HBK, can you tell me what your status is?"

There was an instant crackle, a cluster of broken word sounds, and the line went silent. Arthur frowned, adjusting the dial. "We haven't had issues with this frequency since the storm finally cleared yesterday."

"How is this even working?" She moved next to the equipment.

Arthur pointed to the lithium battery it was connected to as he pressed the button on the speaker again. "Repeat, WA6HBK. There was some interference on our end."

"It's bad, Top." The voice was shaky and electrified by static. "I didn't think it would happen this fast. The riots are out of control. They're burning the city to the ground."

"What city?" Tessa whispered as anxiety raised the hairs on her skin.

"Riverside." Arthur pressed the button. "It's not too late to get out of there."

The silence was punctuated by a short laugh. "You aren't going to do much better, Top. I spoke with WA7BLN this morning and they've got record temps down there in Yuma. People are dying in the streets. It's about the same for N5DRB in El Paso with the riots. We've got confirmation the chain reaches to at least Chicago and they're rumoring it's worldwide."

Arthur's eyes closed, the lines of his face deepening with a heavy sadness. "How are our boys up north doing?"

"Living the dream." There was a heavy sigh on the other end of the line. "Are you heading out soon?"

Arthur glanced sideways at Tessa, choosing his next words carefully and she realized he didn't trust her all that much. Somehow, that stung. "Not today. Sally can't go."

"Give her my love," WA6HBK's voice crackled back. "Hey, I've got to sign off and check the perimeter. The dogs are going wild." Arthur replaced the handheld speaker on the clip and turned the beast of a radio off.

"What was that all about?" Her eyes darted to the stairs.

"Didn't you hear him?" Arthur asked. "It's getting bad everywhere. Days without power and riots are breaking out in the cities. No one can access their money and there is a dwindling supply of food. Do you understand me when I say that things are going to get much worse soon?"

She took a steadying breath. "But we're far enough away from the major cities that it won't be as crazy here, right?"

"That's what I thought when I built this place." He dug his boot into the dirt floor. "But it just kept growing and more people moved in. Now there's too many to take care of. The system is breaking down. Our little hill isn't safe anymore."

"How long until it gets worse?" The words slipped from her lips. She knew this was insane, but the man on the other end of the line had no reason to lie and her father's warning was haunting her.

"Honestly? I don't know." Arthur folded his arms over his chest and stared at her. "Could be hours, could be days, could be a few weeks."

"But in a few weeks the power will be back on so we can just hold out until then." The rationalization brought her comfort. Everything that had happened in the last few days was a raging sea of chaos and she clung to reason like a life vest.

"That's what you're not understanding. The power is not coming back on in a few weeks." The intensity of his statement made her blood run cold. "We'll be lucky if it takes a few months. The government was never prepared for this. There are thousands of fried transformers all over the country right now, and I would assume all over the world. This isn't some nuclear attack, the sun doesn't care about a specific region, every nation is probably facing their own problems. And it takes almost a year to make one of each of these transformers needed to get the power grid back online. There will be no outside aid. No one's coming to help. Until they can figure out how to fix these parts, the world is on its own in the dark. We all are on our own. So, I'll ask you again, how much food do you have?"

Tessa took a step back, her pulse racing through her veins as the walls started closing in. Maybe Arthur was paranoid like her father. *But what if they both are right?*

"My dad said a year. I didn't want to believe him. He told me to bring the kids back home right when all this started." Her foot found the bottom step.

Arthur paused with his hand on the lantern switch. "Where does your father live?"

"A small town in Idaho," she whispered. There was no use holding anything back now. "He's the sheriff there. It's where Landon and I grew up."

"And you didn't go?" Arthur shook his head, trying to understand.

"Not without Landon."

Tears filled Arthur's eyes and she looked away. She didn't need his pity. They stood in silence for a minute and she took the next step up.

"What if he doesn't come back?" He dropped the tone of his voice to hide the emotion in it.

"I'll figure it out then." She climbed the stairs two at a time, trying to outrun the crazy fear that was contained in those cellar walls. Her children's laughter was a soothing sound when she slid open the glass door. Their high-pitched squeals pierced the desert air as they chased each other around the yard burning off their sugar rush. Sally's head whipped to the side, her eyes full of concern, as Tessa stood on the porch with her chest heaving.

"Oh Arthur," she said and patted the step beside her. "Come here and sit with me for a bit."

Tessa stopped herself from screaming for Mason and Emily and dragging them away. The woman's calming presence made that action seem awkward and rude. Besides, in the light of the now normal and setting sun, the crippling fear was beginning to ease. She plopped down beside Sally and put her head in her hands.

"Don't mind him." Sally rubbed Tessa's arm with strong fingers. "Arthur was never good at mincing words. It might not be as bad as all that. You never truly know." Her voice was soothing. Tessa sighed as she sat up straight and looked around their back yard. There was a plastic enclosed greenhouse tucked against the side fence. *How did I never notice that before?*

"I have a gut feeling he is right, but I don't know what to do. Landon is supposed to be home tomorrow."

"And he still might be." Sally smiled. "The kids were telling me all about it. What time are they coming in?"

Tessa blew out a hot breath as she watched Mason trying to teach Emily how to do a cartwheel. Normal words. Normal conversation. This was something to hold on to. "The ombudsman sent an email out Friday morning before all of this," she waved her hand to the sky, "and they said a noon release. Which will probably be closer to two but you know how that goes."

She reached for Tessa's hand and held it within hers. "Are you driving to pick him up?"

"Of course." She nodded. "I've never missed a homecoming."

Sally chewed her bottom lip as her gaze drifted to the yard. "If you want to, you can leave the kids here. It might be a fun surprise for you to bring him home like that."

She voiced the growing fear that was gnawing at Tessa's stomach. She'd have to take the freeways tomorrow and if what they said about the cities was true…

"We'll be okay. I can't leave them alone during this and they are so excited to pick up their dad. I'm trying to keep their life as normal as possible." She knew she was clinging to fraying strands, but no matter how sweet Sally was, she and her husband were still strangers.

Sally held her hand in silence as they sat there on the porch step. Emily tumbled over her feet, falling into the dirt, and Mason helped her upright as he told her to blink the dust away. Emily ran off giggling and Mason tried to catch her.

Sally sighed, squeezing Tessa's hand. "Do you know what you're going to wear?"

8
Tessa

The mattress creaked as Moose stood up and shook the sleep from his bones. Tessa bolted upright in a panic. The warm sunlight coming through the window temporarily blinded her and she squinted as she glanced around the room. Mason and Emily were buried beneath the pillows beside her, oblivious to the pounding of their mother's heart. She cursed as she untangled herself from the blankets. She hadn't meant to fall asleep.

Moose jumped off the bed and brushed himself against her legs. Tessa glared at him. "I'll get you breakfast in a minute, but you have to swear you'll be a great alarm system from here on out if you want to keep earning your meals."

He grunted, lowering his heavy jaw to his paws with his back end and tail wagging playfully in the air. She tried to hide her smile with a stern look, but those big brown eyes broke her resolve.

"Alright. Let's go."

Moose bounded down the stairs in front of her, his steps so loud she wondered how the kids weren't waking up. Then again, they could sleep through gunshots. She gripped the banister in her hand and inhaled a steadying breath. *What's done is done.* No use crying over spilled milk.

Morning dew settled on every surface as the sun's warming rays continued to climb over the mountains. Tessa watched the sun as one might eye a deadly snake. A few days ago, this would be a comforting sight, the light chasing away the dark, but now she found herself consciously aware of each position it took in the sky. It was a silent reminder that the earth was nothing without the guiding star and they were all at her mercy. Supernovas, star's expansions, all the science lessons she'd ignored because the experts assured it wouldn't happen in their lifetimes. If the sun acted like this now, who's to say it wouldn't be worse next year. Or in fifty years. Would her unborn grandchildren be okay?

The kettle screamed as the water boiled on the grill. She turned the burners off. She deserved a hot pot of coffee today and Landon would probably want some when he got home.

Three gallons of water to wash Emily's and then Tessa's hair. Mason had a quick head dunk and shampoo scrub in the bucket. A wet rag to wipe the grime from their bodies and another gallon to rinse them both off quickly in the shower.

Tessa stood in the bathroom alone while Mason and Emily ran off to get clean clothes and she eyed the water in the deep soaking tub wistfully. She wanted to shave her body, scrub every pore of her skin, and feel like a woman again instead of just a mom. She settled for a dry razor and a splash of perfume. At least her hair was drying nice with the relaxing spray she'd worked through it.

"Emily, come here," Tessa called after she'd put on the green silk top and buttoned up her jeans. Emily poked her head around the corner to the bathroom where Tessa stood putting on lip balm and a little bit of mascara.

"How do I look?" Emily spun and curtsied in her chiffon white Christmas dress with lace shawl and bright pink plastic dress up heels.

"You look perfect. Let's fix up those curls." Tessa leaned down to kiss her cheek, letting go of every stubborn thought about telling her to change. Who knew what kind of heart break today would bring? It's better to have hope. *Plastic pink shoes and all.*

"Arthur!" Mason ran through the open garage door down the driveway. Tessa barely had time to clip on the leash before Moose chased after him. Emily's plastic shoes slapped against the concrete and she hurried to not get left behind.

"Slow down, Moose." Tessa tugged on the leash. His tail wagged and he stopped to look at her.

"We're going to pick up my dad," Mason said as he led Arthur up the driveway.

"So I heard." Arthur smiled at Moose who took that as a new best friend introduction and flopped to his back for a belly rub. Arthur kneeled and scratched his fur. "You must not get any love, you old dog."

"He does too," Emily exclaimed. "And he is not old."

Arthur chuckled. "My apologies. He sure puts on a good act."

"I'll say." Tessa sighed. "Here, Mason. Take the leash. You and Emily get him into the truck." Moose's sad brown eyes focused on Tessa and Arthur until the kids coaxed him toward Old Blue. Truck rides stump belly rubs any day.

"You guys okay?" Tessa hugged her arms over her chest as she turned back to Arthur.

He nodded, lowering his face to hide his smile out of respect. "I'm going to need you to stop worrying about us. No matter what happens, we'll be fine. But Sally sent me over to let you know that the offer still stands if you need someone to watch the kids today and I agree with her. We don't know how bad Oceanside is and it might be easier for you to hightail it out of there without the little ones in tow."

"Did Sally really send you over here? Because I think she of all people would understand." Tessa narrowed her eyes.

Arthur looked up to meet her gaze. "No. She told me not to come after she made the offer last night. But I'm worried you aren't thinking clearly and wanted to give you a final chance to see reason. There's a possibility he won't be there."

Tessa turned to look through the windshield of Old Blue. Emily was buckled into her booster seat, Mason sat grinning with his missing tooth smile, and

Moose was behind the steering wheel panting with his pink tongue hanging out of the side of his mouth.

"You don't know what my kids have been through. I know it was harder for you being the service member who deployed and left your family behind, but kids suffer too. They know nothing except this life of disappointment and profound joy when it comes to their dad's career. If there is a chance that they will have happiness today, then I am going to take it. And if I'm wrong, which I feel in my heart I'm not because Landon is coming home, but if I'm wrong then I'll make another plan."

A deep sadness filled his eyes. "We'll be praying for all of you."

"Thank you." Tessa blinked away her tears so her mascara didn't run.

Arthur looked over his shoulder to his house and his gruff voice returned. "I'm curious to see how the base is handling all this anyhow. Come back and let me know."

Tessa cracked a smile and nodded as she turned away. "Expect a full report."

Old Blue rumbled down the steep hill and Tessa's eyes swept the valley below. She wasn't sure what she was expecting to see after Arthur's cryptic cellar conversation yesterday. Maybe the whole world would be in ruins. But it was a quaint and quiet morning with seagulls flying overhead. Turner street was clear. The Suburban had been moved. She slowed

114

down and scanned the houses until she found the vehicle parked in one of the driveways with exhaust coming out of the muffler. She waited to see if it would back up, but it stayed where it was.

I don't want to do this. Tessa put the truck in park and left the engine running. "Sit right here for a second, okay? I'm just going to go say hi and apologize to someone."

There were two people sitting in the front seats but she couldn't make out who they were. She walked up to the tinted driver side window of the Suburban and gave a timid knock against the glass. The window rolled down to expose the woman's face she'd seen the other day flipping her off in the middle of the street. She was painting her nails and watching a show on the iPad plugged in to the dash with another woman in the passenger seat.

"Can I help you?" Realization dawned on the woman's face and her thick lips pressed together into a sneer.

Tessa shifted anxiously. "Hey. I'm sorry to just walk up and disturb you like this. I felt bad about driving off the other day and leaving you stranded there. My kid was in school and I had to rush to pick him up. When I came back, you were gone."

The woman coughed softly, annoyed at the conversation. "We didn't need your help anyway. Charlie's husband and Jed helped push it here when they got home from work." The woman in the passenger seat nodded as she reached for the bottle of nail polish.

Charlie. Charlie. Tessa repeated the name, trying to commit it to memory. "Oh okay, well I'm glad it all worked out." She thrust her hand through the open window. "But my name's Tessa. I live up there on the hill. It's nice to meet you." The woman stared at Tessa's outstretched hand and wiggled her tacky fingers in the air. "Right. My bad." Tessa's hand fell to her side.

"Olivia," the woman said, but didn't return the greeting. She glanced into her rearview mirror. "Looks like your truck is still working though. Are you going somewhere?"

"Just to pick up my husband." She hoped that was the truth.

"The military guy?" Charlie chimed in with a perfectly manicured eyebrow raised. The two women shared a silent look that made Tessa uncomfortable. She was used to women ogling Landon, but she felt like she just stumbled into the hen nest. They already had an idea of who she was and had probably formed an opinion. From the looks of it, it wasn't a good one.

"That's him." Tessa took a step back and gave a short wave. "We've got to take off so we aren't late, but I apologize for the other day and it was nice chatting with you." Olivia nodded and the window rolled up without her speaking another word.

Well that was awful. Tessa climbed behind the steering wheel and put some distance between herself and the subdivision.

Pulling onto the freeway ramp of I-15 proved to be another mistake. None of the stalled cars had been moved from where they died and Old Blue was too big to maneuver around them. Tessa cursed under her breath and watched the rearview mirror as she reversed back down the road.

"Damnit is a bad word Mommy," Emily piped up from her booster seat. Tessa shifted into gear and drove over the grassy field beside the on ramp.

"I know. Don't ever say that word again."

The access road was blocked by a brown crew cab Dodge Ram with its doors and hood left open but no owner in sight. She eased Old Blue off the road to get around it and ended up driving in the ruts for a hundred yards when she was stuck behind a fence.

The local farmer's market stalls and permanent small boutiques store sat boarded up to her right as she drove back onto the road. The sight of the once busy market place so empty and quiet now brought chills down her spine.

A spot of neon yellow flashed through the sparse pine trees on the hill at the end of the access road. When she turned the bend to the open stretch of pavement, the reflective vests of two bicyclists pedaled toward them. Tessa tightened her grip on the wheel as they got closer. Their gear was clean, top of the line, but they were overpacked with their backpacks and trailers as they swerved all over the road. The man in the rear eyed the truck wistfully while she sped past them, but he didn't stop to flag her down.

The access road ended at the top of the hill and Tessa turned right to the overpass. She pulled up to the colorless lights to see how congested the freeway was below them.

"Why are people walking on the road?" Emily laughed. "You can't walk on roads."

"Because their cars are sick." The smile fell from Mason's face. "Right, Mom?"

Tessa stared at the freeway, her fingers tapping against the steering wheel. Southbound was clear except for a few vehicles here and there. She could maneuver the truck around them. But the northbound lanes were a mess. Vehicles bogged down with too many passengers, too many bags, drove slowly around the road blocks. Some were getting out to push the abandoned cars to the side, but most weren't stopping to help. She counted fifteen or so groups of people just walking down the middle of the road pulling carts behind them.

Her stomach clenched as she watched them go and every fiber of her being was telling her to do the same thing, run away from the city by any means possible. Get out before it's too late.

Stop being irrational, she chided herself. Those people probably didn't live there anyway and wanted to go home. If planes weren't flying and public transportation wasn't running, they had to figure out a way to see their family again. Still, she decided to stay away from the freeway if at all possible.

She kept driving past the on ramp and off-roaded down the slope of the mountain side through the sagebrush and dirt toward old highway 395 while the kids cheered her on. Tessa couldn't help but laugh. There was no way Landon was ever going to believe that she was driving like this.

The quiet of the back roads and lack of moving vehicles had Tessa looking over her shoulder, waiting for the flashing lights of a police vehicle to pull them over and ticket her or something for not staying at home. *They'd understand this, wouldn't they?* Once she picked up Landon then she'd stay put unless the military had other plans.

The forested roads gave way to warehouses and tall palm trees that swayed in the gentle sea breeze. She drove onto the 78 and passed through the industrial district. Tessa cranked down the window as they got closer to the ocean. The humid air and lack of AC in the truck was making sweat bead on her skin.

"Watch out, Mom!" Mason cried.

She jerked the wheel too hard making the tires skid on the asphalt on the highway near the private airfield. The power steering was awful and she had to pull hard to right the course.

"What was it?" Tessa asked breathlessly as she slammed on the brakes and checked the mirrors. A woman with dyed blue hair and a lip full of piercings waved her fist in the air as she pulled a rolling suitcase toward the tarmac.

"I'm sorry. I didn't see her," Tessa stuttered. She reached for Mason's hand and pulled him close.

Emily was singing her own little tune, lost in the excitement of the day.

"Something's not right," he whispered so quietly against the silk of her shirt that she felt the words more than heard them.

"I know." Tessa kissed the top of his head. "But we're going to be okay and I promise you'll be safe."

Mason pulled himself from the embrace and sat up on his knees. His breath was hot against Tessa's ear as he whispered, "What if Dad isn't there?"

He glanced nervously at Emily and Tessa's heart caught in her throat when she realized the silent burden her son had been carrying all alone in his little head. Tears threatened to spill from her eyes. It was so hard to remember that the boy who cried about melting popsicles and ran around in underwear pretending to be a superhero was becoming more aware of adult problems every day.

She smoothed back his hair, staring into his eyes as he looked to her for reassurance. "When the power goes out, a lot of things can happen."

"Like cars get sick," Emily said, suddenly present in the moment.

Tessa cringed and inhaled deeply. "When a big, big thing makes the power go out, lots of things can happen. It seems like some cars can get sick. The water can stop flowing from the sink. Our food doesn't stay cold in the fridge anymore. And sometimes things won't happen like we want them to."

"So Dad might not be coming home." Mason closed his eyes and fell back against the seat.

She didn't want to do this. Not now when they still had hope. The speech about delayed deployments like the one when Mason was four and how they had to be brave like always died upon her lips. Emily twisted her ankles to admire her shoes and Mason's shoulders sagged as he waited for the blow to come. In the blink of an eye, he'd grown old enough that keeping hard truths from him would do more harm than good. She hated herself for not seeing it sooner, for still clinging to the last days of magic when he wanted to hear the truth. *Is Santa coming next?*

"I don't know," Tessa said. "We are supposed to pick him up and I haven't been able to get in touch with anyone who would tell me otherwise. If he's not there, then we'll find out where he is and how much longer we have to wait."

The kids were silent, lost in their own thoughts, and it broke her heart to know that she'd crushed theirs. She ruffled the top of Mason's hair. "But we don't know that yet, so stop worrying until we do."

He lifted his face and smiled. "There's my boy." She pinched his cheek. Moose gave a low growl and jumped up between the kids barking just as Tessa glanced over to the passenger side window to see a man standing right outside, inches away from Emily. He dug in his pocket making eye contact with Tessa. She held in a strangled cry as she shifted into drive.

"Wait." The man hit his palm against the window and Mason let go of Moose's collar as he jumped onto Emily's lap still barking. Tessa floored it, kicking up rocks at the business man who stood waving his wallet in the cloud of dust they left behind.

"Who was that?" Emily grunted, pushing Moose off her lap and back onto the floorboard.

"A strange man." Tessa kept her focus on the road and her hands tight on the wheel to stop them from shaking.

"We don't talk to strangers," Emily whispered. She closed her eyes and started to sing. Mason reached over to grab her hand and a single tear slid down Tessa's cheek.

What is happening now?!

Tessa slammed on the brakes. The 78 spit them out on a sharp right turn under the overpass of I-5 and it was a short drive up the hill to get to the main gate of base, but she couldn't move past the tunnel. If seeing no people in once crowded places was scary, this many of them where there shouldn't be any was terrifying. She hesitated. Her hand hovered above the drive shaft and she wanted to throw it in reverse and escape, but other than a few curious glances, no one seemed to care about the truck being there.

But she couldn't get any closer and see the gate without plowing through the mass of bodies. She backed up to the gas station and put the truck in park.

"I want to get Daddy," Emily whined as she kicked her plastic shoes against the dashboard.

"Let me think," Tessa snapped, and instantly regretted it when Emily started to cry. She reached for her and rubbed a soothing hand along her arm. "There's a lot of people out there and I don't think they are letting anyone in."

"Can we go check?" Mason asked, the last bit of hope fading from his eyes.

Tessa bit her lip and nodded. "Alright baby, let's go see."

She took the keys from the ignition and shoved them in her pocket, leaning over to unbuckle Emily as she locked the passenger side door. Emily scrambled across the seat clinging to her mother's neck. "Hold my hand and don't let go." She squeezed Mason's fingers. He nodded, not daring to speak. Emily kept her legs wrapped around Tessa's waist as she climbed down from the truck.

"Stay here bud." Tessa pushed Moose's thick head back into the truck as she locked the door and closed it behind them.

The putrid smell of unwashed bodies and the gut-wrenching sound of babies crying tore at her heart while she pushed her way through the crowd.

"Mom?" Mason gasped as she pulled him past a veteran in a wheelchair who was missing both legs and had a blood-soaked and dirt crusted gauze wrapped around his head. She wanted to help him, but she couldn't with the kids here. Emily buried her face against Tessa's chest and started to hum.

"Close your eyes," Tessa whispered, forcing her way closer to the gate.

"I have an ID Card, let me in!" a man screamed from her left, jumping to be higher than the crowd.

"We all have ID cards," a woman's shrill voice screamed from somewhere to the right.

There was a break in the crowd where the shoulders shifted enough to let Tessa see the gate. The entrance was sealed off with metal barricades and there were guard towers erected over the high arch of the structure with rifles pointed at the people gathered outside. *This cannot be happening.* Tessa pulled against Mason's hand, backtracking their previous steps. No one was getting in through that set up and she didn't want to stick around with the growing mob to figure out why.

"My shoe!" Emily cried and launched herself out of Tessa's arm. Tessa lunged for her, trying to scoop her up in the chaos while crushing the bones of Mason's hand.

"There are children out here! You have to let us in." A frantic woman twice Tessa's size with long blond dreadlocks grabbed Emily and lifted her into the air.

"Let go of my daughter!" Tessa screamed as she ripped at the woman's back, grabbing a handful of the rope like locks and yanking down so the woman's head was level with her spine. She released her grip on Emily and tried to spin around to face Tessa. But Tessa swept her daughter into her arms and took off running, dragging Mason by his hand before the woman could stand up straight.

"My shoes." Snot poured down Emily's face as she sobbed against Tessa's shirt. More people were coming down from the exit ramp on the freeway, filing in like cattle towards the gate. Tessa pushed past them as she fought her way back through the growing crowd. Blood pounded in her ears and Mason's hand was slick in hers. She adjusted her grip and yanked him through the tunnel and down the road toward the waiting truck.

Mason flattened himself against the door, looking wild-eyed in every direction as Tessa fumbled with the keys. Moose was barking like crazy with spit flying from his massive jaws. Some of the people coming down from the freeway thought better of their plan and turned towards the gas station instead. She didn't wait to see what they were doing.

"Help her get buckled," Tessa demanded as she shoved both kids inside the truck. Mason clicked Emily in and Tessa gunned it. The tires screeched as she sped across the parking lot.

"I want Daddy!" Emily was hysterical, snot and tears soaked her blotchy red face.

"I'm sorry," Tessa choked out. "Mommy made a mistake." Moose sighed and rested his jaw on Mason's lap. Hot tears rolled silently down the boy's cheeks.

"A lot of people are trying to get on base and it's too much for the gate guards to handle so we'll come back another time or Daddy will come to us." She had to stop to breathe. *Fix this for them somehow.*

"Can you guys sing me a song? I'm in the mood for some rock and roll."

The kids were a stunned shade of passive as Tessa pulled into the driveway. A few rounds of her offkey singing the classics had elicited some giggles from them and made Emily stop crying, but the final quiet mile through the subdivision where curtains were closed on curious neighbors as they peeked out of their windows when Old Blue rumbled by was the final pull of emotions for the day. They could sense her defeat and she knew it.

"Pancakes for dinner?" Tessa asked, trying to bring the smiles back to their faces. Mason nodded, scratching Moose behind the ear, and Emily said nothing as she walked barefoot with her shawl dragging on the floor into the house.

"I'll be right in." Tessa motioned for Moose to follow Mason inside. The dog hesitated, staring at her with his soulful eyes and tail wagging. "Go," she whispered and turned her back to him so the kids wouldn't see her break. The click of the door closing brought tears that blurred her vision and her chest tightened as she struggled to breathe.

She took the few steps outside, sucking in air and willing herself to calm down. *Get it together. You don't have another choice.* If Landon wasn't coming, she had to get the kids out of here and somewhere safe. She needed to take them back home. Gravel crunched on the road and Tessa angrily wiped her hands over her eyes, but there was no way to hide the absolute wreck she'd become.

"How bad is it?" Arthur kept a respectful distance, standing in the street and not looking directly at her face.

"It's bad." Fresh tears sprung to her eyes. "There were maybe forty people and fifteen cars I counted this morning coming up north on I-15. It was double that number this afternoon. The main gate to base is overrun. It's like everyone with an ID card is trying to get in and they locked it all down. I didn't stay long enough to figure out why." Her voice cracked and she ground her teeth to stop from screaming out the next words, "Someone grabbed Emily."

"Is she okay?" He stepped closer with his fists clenched at his side. The instant concern for some child he just met made the guilt she felt so much worse.

Tessa lowered her face. "She's fine. But I really messed up. I didn't want to believe Landon isn't coming back."

"Why don't you go talk to Sally? I'll stay with the kids while you take some time to sort things out," Arthur said softly.

"I'll be alright." She straightened her chin and wiped the tears from her eyes. "They need me and I can't leave them."

He glanced down at his worn boots and sighed. "This is a hard situation, but I want to believe he's coming home for all your sakes."

"Maybe he'll still come home tonight. He can get a ride from someone." She tried to sound hopeful but the words were hollow in her ears.

"Maybe. You come let us know if you need anything in the meantime, okay?"

Tessa nodded, holding her arms across her chest to keep herself together as she went to go start making dinner.

Her thoughts wouldn't stop racing. Even as the kids slept peacefully in her bed and Moose's loud snores echoed in the quiet room, she couldn't turn her mind off to sleep. Every creak of the house, the slight shift of the wind rustling through the cracks in the windows, set her back on high alert. She prayed that every sound was Landon and imagined she could hear the turn of the key in the lock. But when she glanced down at Emily's thick eyelashes fluttering with childlike dreams, she knew she couldn't afford to think like this much longer.

The bed groaned when she climbed out of it and she stood waiting in the moonlight for one of the kids to stir. Finally, her shoulders relaxed and she reached for the pistol. Moose opened one lazy eye to see if it was breakfast time.

"Stay," she whispered and closed the door softly behind her.

9

Landon

"Hey Doc, you missed breakfast." Sgt. Sierra moved out of the way to let Landon pass. The ship groaned as it was rocked from side to side on the waves, metal creaking in protest from sitting still for too long.

"Yeah, I was trying to send an email but comms are still down." He kept his tone even so as not to let the frustration of the past hour he'd spent slamming letters on the keyboard show.

"That sucks," Sgt. Sierra groaned. "I was just heading that way. My girlfriend was supposed to fly in from Texas for homecoming. She's going to be so pissed. Twenty bucks says she breaks up with me now."

Landon's shoulders stiffened as he forgot his own problems for a blissful minute. "I'm sure everything will be alright, but I'm here if you want to talk about it."

Sgt. Sierra chuckled. "Nah, man. I'm good. Save the wizard hat for the other guys. Today's going to be a rough one. Let me know if you need any help."

Landon finished the granola bar from the last care package he'd received and closed his wall locker just as LCpl Wallis poked her head into the berthing.

"Hey HM2. I hit my hand and something is wrong with it."

"Let me see." Landon met her at the door. She held out her purple bruised and swollen thumb. The edges of fading yellow discoloration spread down to her wrist, the nail bed was raised with a blood blister underneath, and she flinched when he pushed against the finger pad. "When did you do this?"

"A couple of days ago." She shrugged.

He released her hand. "And you're just telling me now."

"I figured I'd go to the ER when we got home if it got any worse." She cradled her arm to her chest and avoided his stare.

"What exactly did you do?" Landon folded his arms and waited for the truth.

"I, uh." She looked away. "I slammed it in the taxi door when we were in port."

Landon laughed. "How drunk were you?"

"I made it back on ship, didn't I?"

"Come on." He shook his head. "Let's get you to medical and get it checked out."

Chief Elyse was leaning against CDR Jenkins desk and going over notes with him when Landon entered with Wallis in tow. "Morning Commander. Morning Chief." He nodded in their direction. Chief

Elyse gave her signature hate filled scowl as she gathered up the reports.

CDR Jenkins leaned back on his rolling chair and looked Landon over, reading his name plate silently. "HM2 Ward. Were you the one who brought in Martinez the other day?"

"He was already here, sir," Landon explained. "I just came to check on him and left the request for meds from you with the HN who was here on duty."

"Good call." CDR Jenkins nodded. "Make sure you check on him today. What do we have going on here?"

"Blunt force trauma to the left thumb." Landon motioned for LCpl Wallis to take a seat on the patient bed.

"How'd that happen?" CDR Jenkins rolled his stool over to get a closer look. Wallis's eyes were pleading as she stared at Landon and CDR Jenkins manipulated her finger to check for a break.

"Coffin rack mishap." Landon turned and searched through the medical cart for some tape.

"Has anyone seen Martinez?" Landon poked his head into Charlie Company's berthing.

"Yeah, he was in the mess deck at lunch," Cpl Hemming said in a thick southern drawl. Landon's stomach growled, reminding him that he'd missed two meals today. After LCpl Wallis's thumb was wrapped up, he was caught in the passageway by a

Marine with a nose bleed and had to turn around to take him to medical.

"Did he seem okay?" Landon asked.

"He's as upset as everyone else." Cpl Hemming packed his dip can and twisted off the lid. "But he wasn't breaking down crying like he did the other day if that's what you mean."

Landon sighed, running his hand over his head. "Alright, tell him I'm looking for him if you see him."

He stopped by his wall locker on the way back out and emptied the box of the last granola bar that was left. The bar had crumbled in the bag. He opened it from the top and poured the grains into his mouth. Tessa always sent this health food crap in packages now. It wasn't always this way. In the early days the care boxes were full of cheese whiz and candy. But the garbage on ship and too many MREs were taking their toll on his gut and he knew this was her way of saying she cared. *When I get home, I'm grilling some big, juicy steaks.*

Landon pulled out the folded letter that came with the box on their last mail drop. It was only a short love note, but he read through it again. This was a better message than the last email she'd sent. He focused on those three words "I love you," knowing those were the ones she really meant. Whatever happened that night she emailed him wasn't important.

"Not you too." Sgt. Sierra peeked over Landon's shoulder. His elbow jerked back reflexively, but he caught himself before he knocked Sierra to the deck.

"Dude, don't sneak up on people like that." Landon folded the letter and tucked it away.

Sgt. Sierra chuckled. "Sorry to interrupt your me time, Doc, but have you seen Martinez anywhere? Chief Elyse stopped me in the hanger bay asking about him."

"Why is she getting involved in this? I was looking for him earlier but couldn't find him either."

Sgt. Sierra blew out a heavy breath. "Guess we get to play hide-n-seek."

"Yeah." Landon closed his locker, a sense of urgency pushing him forward. "Guess so."

They searched the berthing and the mess deck before climbing to the hanger bay. Each shake of the head when they asked if anyone had seen Martinez brought a cold sweat down Landon's back. Sgt. Sierra organized two more search teams of privates and lance corporals. They didn't want to get Martinez in trouble with the higher enlisted if this was some kind of misunderstanding, but every second that ticked by was a second closer to the inevitable.

"Hey, I heard you're missing a guy." HM3 Cooper bumped into Landon as he climbed down the ladder well to retrace his steps. "And Chief Elyse is looking for both of you."

Landon cursed under his breath. "If you see her, let her know that I'll bring Martinez up to medical as soon as I grab him."

He checked the berthing again, pulling back every curtain to make sure Martinez wasn't asleep somewhere he shouldn't be and then backtracked toward the mess deck, searching each Marine's face as they passed in the corridor. His pulse was racing, blood thrumming against his eardrums, but he tried not to give in to the rising panic as he kept asking if anyone had seen him.

"Someone's crying in the head," a corporal mentioned in the passageway when Landon stopped him. He looked over his shoulder, locking eyes with Sgt. Sierra, and both men took off running.

Time slowed and Landon could feel each pounding beat of his heart as he ripped open the hatch to the head. His boots slapped against the damp floors when he raced inside. "Martinez!" It was too quiet, soul crushing quiet, and his voice echoed back to him from the steel walls.

"Did you find him?" Sgt. Sierra called out breathlessly. Landon didn't stop to answer. An empty mop bucket skid out from the shower stall, the hollow thump as it rolled over ringing too loud in the silent room.

"Martinez!" Landon screamed and lunged forward. He caught the sway of the corporal's body mid-swing as it dangled from the pipe above the showers with the repel rope wrapped around his neck. His muscles screamed in protest as he hoisted Martinez above his head to release the tension.

"Cut the rope and get him down," he cried through clenched teeth and shifted the weight of the body onto his shoulders and his head. Sgt. Sierra grabbed the bucket and turned it upright, using his pocket knife to saw at the fibers of the rope.

"He's clear, Doc."

Landon didn't feel the release, but he lowered Martinez now, cradling him in his arms as if he were a child. He glanced up at Sgt. Sierra's tear-streaked face and felt the moisture on his own cheeks.

"What happened?" A crowd of Marines were gathering around, filling the small space.

Landon laid Martinez on the deck and his fingers moved swiftly to find the corporal's steady pulse. Anger welled inside of him, turning his vision red. He grabbed Martinez by his shoulders. "What the hell is wrong with you?" Martinez's eyes flew open and he started to cough, but the words continued to rush from Landon's lips, "This is how you want your kid to remember you? You would leave her, leave your family like this? They need you."

"Doc, are you okay?" Sgt. Sierra dropped to his knees and placed his hand on Landon's back. LCpl Martinez stared up wide-eyed from the shower floor, seeing everything and saying nothing.

"I'm fine." Landon shoved him off as he checked the neck for swelling and watched for the even rise and fall of the lance corporal's chest. "Help me get him up and take him to medical. Martinez, can you walk?" The lance corporal looked at him blankly, but there were no physical signs that he couldn't speak.

"You're fine," Landon snapped. "Are you going to make us carry you?"

Martinez coughed, pushing himself to his elbows. "No HM2. I can walk."

His fists stayed clenched at his sides as he marched the patient through the ship. He should have called in a medical emergency. He should have found him sooner. *I'm going to be in deep sh…*

"You got this?" Sgt. Sierra fell behind as they got closer to medical. Landon nodded and he slipped away.

"I'm sorry," Martinez whispered. His face was covered with a sickly sheen of sweat. "I didn't know what else to do."

Landon swallowed back his anger and tried to sound more compassionate. "It was a dumb plan. We all miss our families, but how can you take care of them if you're dead?"

"They're going to discharge me now, aren't they?" His breath hitched in his throat and he started backing up toward the bulkhead, reaching for something to cling to.

Landon grabbed his shoulders and forced the lance corporal to focus before his panic got out of control. "It'll be okay if they do. You won't have to live like this anymore."

"Will they tell my wife what happened?" He tried to slow down and breathe.

"No." Landon guided him toward the hatch. "And we'll get you all the help you need."

Chief Elyse was the first to jump from her seat. Her eyes were bloodshot, shooting daggers into his soul. GySgt. Fuimaono and SSgt. Richards stood behind CDR Jenkins. Their shoulders were tense and stress radiated through the room. Landon hung his head, waiting for the storm that was coming. He'd hoped to be the first to tell them, but the rumors moved faster than they could walk.

"Take a seat." He motioned for the lance corporal to move to the open patient bed.

"Doc?" Martinez called out in a small voice.

"Think of it like a vacation," Landon whispered. "I promise you'll be okay." CDR Jenkins slid over and pulled off his stethoscope to start taking vitals.

"HM2 Ward," Chief Elyse spit his name and turned on her heel to leave. "Come with me."

"And when you get done here, report to my office." GySgt. Fuimaono flexed his arms and Landon tried not to flinch. *Great.*

He clenched his teeth, staring straight ahead and coming to attention as Senior Chief Miller closed the door to the surgical room behind him.

Chief Elyse was seething as she paced back and forth. "Commander Jenkins gave you a direct order to check on a patient this morning and you failed to follow through. Want to tell me what you were doing instead?"

Taking care of other patients, Landon didn't say. "I was searching for him, but I stopped for a minute to get a snack and read a letter. It was my fault I didn't find him sooner. I should have kept looking instead."

"To read a letter?" Her nostrils flared.

"Just a quick one, Chief." He knew he shouldn't have mentioned it, but he didn't want to lie.

"I don't care how quick it was," she yelled. "You had a mentally unstable patient that you failed to care for and from my understanding, a minute later and the outcome would have been much different."

"I understand the severity of this." Landon lowered his eyes. "Like I said, this is my fault and I accept one hundred percent of the blame. I'll take whatever punishment you want to give me."

Her face twisted into a sneer as she kept pacing and he waited for the blow to come.

"Get out of my sight."

He didn't need to be told twice.

His stomach growled in protest as he walked straight to GySgt. Fuimaono's office, but he didn't dare stop at the mess deck. He'd been too lucky with Chief Elyse, though he expected her wrath to manifest over the coming days. She was like Tessa in that way, short and full of hellfire, and they both could hold a grudge. Thinking about his wife made the hunger worse, so he buried it deep inside as he raised his fist to knock on the hatch.

"Come in," GySgt. Fuimaono's heavy voice commanded loud enough to be heard through layers of metal that separated each compartment. Landon hardened his face, steeling himself for the second round of the night.

"HM2 Ward," SSgt Richards growled as soon as Landon stepped inside. "You want to explain to me why one of my Marines almost killed himself today?"

"He has medical issues, Staff Sergeant. But they've intensified in light of the news about homecoming." Landon twisted the ring on his finger behind his back, drawing strength from it.

SSgt. Richard's square face turned bright red. If the Marine mascot was a bulldog, this man was the embodiment. "You were told to be on watch for situations like this."

"I was and I failed." The words tasted bitter on his tongue and the guilt weighed heavy on his shoulders. "I promise not to fail again."

"I don't want your promises." SSgt. Richards kicked back his chair and thrust his pointed hand in the air. Landon lowered his face, torn between wanting to defend himself and knowing he was responsible for this.

"That's enough, Staff Sergeant," GySgt. Fuimaono's voice was low and full of threat. "Leave us now." SSgt. Richards looked over his shoulder, but a quick narrow of the gunnery sergeant's dark brown eyes sent him marching out of the office.

The absence of SSgt. Richard made GySgt. Fuimaono seem larger, more terrifying, as he watched him with his eyebrow raised. Landon could feel the judgment coming. He did his best to stand steady with a thousand-yard stare directed at the bulkhead under the weight of it.

"Sit down." GySgt. Fuimaono sighed.

"Gunny?" Landon's eyes darted to the giant's face, wondering if this was some sort of trick.

"I said sit down." GySgt. Fuimaono pulled out a chair and laid his massive forearms on the table. "Tell me what really happened."

Landon took the edge of the seat with his back straight as if he was still standing at attention. "LCpl Martinez has had some anxiety issues in the past. His wife is due with their first child any day. He had a panic attack and I thought I got him the right treatment and requested he be sent for further evaluation when we got home, but I failed him."

GySgt. Fuimaono nodded, taking it all in. "Your job is to keep my Marines healthy. I know that can be a lot to ask sometimes, but if you can't perform your duties than you don't belong here. Do you really feel that you failed?"

Landon didn't know the answer to that and the insinuation that he couldn't do his job sliced through him like a knife. "I should have done better."

"And I believe you will next time." He smiled, a short curve of his upper lip changing his stern face into something else entirely for a moment before the mask slipped back into place. "It seems you have some Marines that care about you and wanted to make sure your name was in the clear. You were in Sangin on your first tour, right?"

Sierra. Landon clenched his jaw. "Our unit came in towards the end. We missed most of it."

GySgt. Fuimaono nodded and didn't press further. "Alright. Go hit the rack. It's been a long day for everyone."

"How bad was it?" Sgt. Sierra poked his head out from his bunk.

Landon leaned down to unlace his boots. "Could have been worse, I guess. But don't fight my battles for me."

"Who me? I didn't do anything." He laughed. "But you have to know this wasn't your fault, man. There's no way any of us would have guessed he would take it that far." Sgt. Sierra rolled over and propped himself up on his forearm, but Landon wasn't in the mood to talk.

He lifted himself onto the thin mattress and bunched the pillow under his head. The day's events played out in his mind on repeat, every second he wasted and the things he should have done differently. The guilt of it all made him physically sick and the rocking of the ship didn't help with the discomfort.

Landon closed his eyes and tried to will the feeling away. Sleep was just out of reach. Every time he could sense it coming, it would fade with another worry. He tried to focus on memories of Tessa and the kids, bright spots in the dark and clustered space. Emily's giggles. Mason's smile. Moose drooling over the baseball. The curve of Tessa's neck when he pressed his lips against it.

"You feel that, Doc?" Sgt. Sierra's voice drifted to him as a whisper. Landon's eyes shot open and he laid as still as he could in the quiet of the night. The rocking of the ship had eased, smoothing to a steadier rhythm. They were moving again.

I'm going home.

The plastic doll arm stabbed like a sharp rock as it crunched under Tessa's foot. She brought her knee to her chest, hopping away from the offensive toy and pressing her lips together to stop the long string of curse words from flowing out as the pain subsided. When it was just a dull ache, she stepped carefully through Emily's dark room and dug in the closet for the sequined unicorn backpack with the purple straps that the girl had never used.

Downstairs, she dropped Emily's bag next to Mason's school backpack on the entry way bench and turned on the camping lantern so it cast a warm glow over her notebook on the kitchen counter. She needed to get serious, needed a more long-term plan in case Landon never came home.

He is coming home. She ripped out the page of things she *might* need and balled it up in her fist. He would be back; it was only a matter of when. The problem was if they could wait that long. Guilt from that last email dug its claws into her heart and twisted. She furiously clicked on the cam of the pen, willing the tears away.

The drive to her dad's normally took twenty hours, but that was before the way the roads looked now with abandoned vehicles and foot traffic. *Maybe a week now?* She'd plan for two and hope it would take much less. Gas was the major issue. There was a full can in the garage, but they were going to need more than that. Would anyone care if she siphoned it out of the vehicles left on the road? She glanced down at the stupid pink pistol on the counter next to her.

At least when she got out of Southern California it would be mostly empty highways through the Nevada desert. But what if they broke down somewhere with no way to call for help?

Focus. She forced herself to breathe. If she kept worrying about the what ifs, she'd drive herself insane. It was safer at her dad's house. Larry still had his ranch next door. There was the river for water and she couldn't remember if her dad still had chickens, but she could probably get some baby chicks from Larry's wife. She'd take all the food she had. Start a garden when she got there. But first things first, she had to pack.

After she'd scribbled down a list of things they were taking with them, the anxiety eased and her eyelids grew heavy. She needed to decide when to leave, but she could do that in the light of day.

Tessa dragged the chair over to the hallway closet where the extra throw blankets for the couch were stowed on the top shelf. Her hand brushed against Landon's fleece lined jacket that was still hanging in the spot she had put it when she'd unpacked the house. Tears blurred her vision as she pulled it from the hanger and brought it against her face, inhaling whatever fading scents that were left of her husband.

She could see him wearing it last winter when they'd chopped down the Christmas tree at the farm and then again in early spring when there was a freak snowstorm in North Carolina and he'd dragged the kids around on sleds until their noses were bright red.

"See if mama will make us some hot chocolate." The smile on his face when he noticed her watching.

Her chest tightened and a hard lump swelled in her throat. She carried the jacket over to the couch and then pulled her knees to her chest as she wrapped it around her entire body. Her hands found the too big arm holes and she snuggled into them, resting her head against the fabric and crying softly until the sun rose.

Moose came bounding into the kitchen ahead of Mason and slid across the tile floor until his nose smacked into the back of Tessa's knee. She reached down to scratch behind his ear with one hand and flipped sausages in the skillet with the other. The deep freezer was losing the last of its cold fast so a stack of sausages and some fruit sounded like a healthy enough breakfast and lunch.

"Morning Mom." Mason slid onto his chair at the table. She glanced over her shoulder to give him a smile, but his back was turned to her with his head resting on his arms. Moose issued a single demanding bark.

"Guess you want breakfast too." She scooped out a cup of dog food from the plastic bin and paused, staring at the remaining kibble. His next shipment of food was scheduled for later this week and the realization that it wasn't coming was the final nail in the coffin. She had enough left for another two weeks, maybe three if she could stretch it.

"How about sausage for breakfast?" she asked, dropping the cup back into the bin. Moose's ears perked up and he wagged his tail as he padded over to his rug to wait.

"Am I going to school today?" Mason's voice was barely a whisper.

Tessa turned off the flame and moved the pan from the burner. "Not today. The power is still out."

"Ah man." Mason sighed.

"That's a first." She laughed as she fixed up the plates. "Since when are you bummed about missing school?" He looked up at the single remaining blue construction paper chain still hanging from the hook and didn't speak. Tessa's heart broke all over again.

"I'm awake." Emily came skipping to the table with a Barbie doll tucked under her arm. Tessa glared at the toy, remembering the pain one of its kin had caused her last night. Emily wrapped her slender arms around her waist for a hug. Tessa tilted her chin up to check for any signs of permanent damage and was greeted with a wide and wondering smile.

"What's wrong?" Emily pulled her face away from Tessa's hand.

"Nothing." She shook her head. "Breakfast is ready."

Mason chewed silently and avoided making eye contact with anyone while Moose wolfed down his sausages and wagged his tail for another. Tessa wasn't hungry anyway so she set her plate on the floor.

"Alright guys, here's what I'm thinking for today." She clapped her hands together in front of her chest. "Mason, you're going to pick out a book and read it aloud to me, then write down any words you need help pronouncing…"

"Oh, come on," he groaned.

"Ah," she held her finger in the air, "don't interrupt. You were the one who was sad about missing school so we're going to get some homework done. And Emily," Tessa zeroed in on her daughter and the girl gulped, "you are going to pick up every single Barbie from every floor in this house and put them in the bin in your room." Emily nodded. She could do that.

Tessa looked back to Mason who was pushing the strawberries around on his plate and doing his best not to cry. "And as soon as you both finish all that, we'll go over to Sally and Arthur's house to visit." Mason cracked a small smile. It was enough to ease her guilt and give her courage for the next words she had to say. "How do you two feel about taking a trip to see Grandpa soon?"

"Grandpa," Emily shrieked. Of course she would be excited, it wasn't Tessa or Landon that sent a new Barbie to her doorstep every month.

"But what about Dad?" Mason's smile didn't reach his eyes. She leaned across the table and clasped his hand in hers, hoping to give comfort and reassurance that she was struggling to maintain for herself.

"If Dad isn't home by the time we leave, then he knows where Grandpa's house is and he will meet us there."

The sound of a motor starting reached them before they made it past the hedges. Four days ago, she wouldn't have paid any attention to the noise but now it seemed out of place. Arthur was backing a utility ATV out of the shed at the side of the house and Tessa couldn't believe how loud it was. *Old Blue must sound like a tank.* He drove it over to the garage and killed the engine.

"Take off your shoes and don't break anything," Tessa called out as the kids raced past Arthur and into the house.

"They'll be okay." He chuckled. "Sally's making brownies. Perfect timing. She was going to have me walk them over to you this afternoon."

Their thoughtfulness was too much, but she was grateful to have met them and that statement alone was enough to solidify what she wanted to say to them both today.

"What are you doing with that thing?" Tessa motioned to the ATV as they walked up onto the porch.

Arthur wiped the dirt from his hands on his pants and scanned the hill around them before stepping inside. "I'm going to clear the brush for a 200ft perimeter. Been meaning to do it for a while now." The smell of freshly baked brownies made her mouth water and her feet took her to the kitchen before she had the chance to ask why in the world he'd want to do that.

Sally held up a small white plate with a perfectly cut square of chocolate heaven and handed it to Tessa with her blue eyes beaming with motherly warmth.

"Thank you." She inhaled it in two bites. The kids had already run out back and Tessa turned to watch them through the glass. They had a full yard of toys at home and still preferred the dirt lot with its single tire swing hanging from the gnarly pine that overlooked the valley below.

"How are you doing?" Sally rubbed Tessa's arm. "Arthur told me about what happened at base."

Tessa patted her hand and then put her plate in the sink. "I'll be okay, but I've got to take care of a few things and then I think we need to make a trip up to Idaho to stay with my dad until this all blows over."

"Idaho?" Sally's face fell. "Do you really think it's safe to travel right now?"

"Honestly? I think we should have left days ago. If what Arthur says is true, the roads are only going to get worse as more people leave the cities. Who knows what it will be like next week?"

"And Landon?" Sally asked the question softly, without accusation or implying hope.

Still, Tessa wanted to cry, feeling judgement when she knew there was none. "Landon would want us to be safe."

"About that," Sally leaned onto her cane, "I think you and Arthur and I need to sit down to have a serious talk. I'm not telling you to stay if your heart is set on going, but I will tell you there are options."

"Options?" Tessa arched an eyebrow.

"The brownies are getting cold," Sally's voice rang out through the house and Arthur shuffled into the kitchen.

"We can't have that." He stooped down to kiss her cheek. "I just went to wash my hands."

"As I was saying," Sally playfully swatted him away, "if you saw a few hundred people on the freeway yesterday then that must only be the first wave. There are over a million people in San Diego alone and sooner or later they are going to want to get out of the city. We're far enough off the beaten path to not be a target to most of them, but not everyone will be content with just passing through."

Tessa bit her lip. "All the more reason for us to leave soon. If we need to get out of here, I'd rather be ahead of the mass exodus and not in the middle of it. And I actually came over here today to tell you both that you should come with us. Moose City doesn't have much, but it's self-reliant and my dad is the sheriff up there. Plus, it's small enough that no one even knows it exists."

"If that's the case maybe you would be better off for the long term back home." Sally pulled a cloth from her pocket and dabbed it against her eyes. "But I don't think I can make a journey like that right now." Arthur stopped chewing and put his plate on the counter.

"Now don't you start," Sally cut him off before he could get a word in. "I told you what I was going to say and you will let me finish." Arthur nodded, picking up his discarded plate, and Tessa tried not to laugh.

"Like I said," Sally continued. "I don't blame you if you want to go, but if you want to stay then you have some options. Arthur and I have been preparing for a situation like this all our adult lives and I'm confident we can weather the storm no matter how long it lasts. I've made a list of some ideas and we can sit down to discuss them together. Defending two properties might be a bit tricky, but I was thinking we can work out some sort of plan. An easier option would be if you and the kids stayed here temporarily…"

"Slow down." Tessa held up her hand. "When you say you've been planning for this, it makes me a little nervous. Planning for what exactly?"

Sally's gaze drifted to the backyard. "We planned for everything. At first it was a parent's instinct. We wanted to keep Anissa safe in case some major crisis were to happen, but the more we learned about preparedness, the more we planned."

Doomsday preppers. End of the world junkies. She thought of all the labeled bins in the cellar and knew exactly what these words meant. There was a time she would have thought it was crazy, but with every passing moment of this changing world the conversation about survival suddenly seemed like the most rational thing to have. She felt small and unprepared, like all her lists and worry and simple plans weren't enough to keep her family safe.

"I only have another twenty-six days of food for the kids. Less than that if I feed Moose. There's some chicken and the last of the frozen vegetables melting in the deep freezer as we speak. I found a few cases of MREs in the garage, but I don't even know if they're expired. I don't have enough to stay here and help you out if this is going to last a long time." She wanted to take the words back, to scoop them up and live in an alternate reality where she planned for longer. Where she wasn't a charity case standing in Sally's kitchen.

Arthur dropped his plate into the sink. His back was to her as he spoke, "That's how we started too. Thirty days of food and a plan to get some more. Enough ammo to last a while and a list of what we needed to do next. We don't think you are ill prepared. You are only starting out, but you have the right mindset to survive and that's why you have options now."

He turned to give her a smile. "Besides, it doesn't matter what the date is on the MRE bags. Those things never expire."

Tessa chuckled, the possibilities running through her mind, but a small voice of reason held her tongue in check. She would say yes in an instant if there was proof that Landon was coming back, but without knowing what was going to happen, her priority was to protect her kids. Sally and Arthur were nice enough—too nice some would argue—and she was sure they weren't offering help for nothing. They needed another set of eyes on the dead-end road, another gun at the ready. That was all understandable, but what if something happened to her? These people would be the only things standing between the chaos of the city or the possibility of starvation and her kids.

"I have to think about this," she said.

"Take all the time you need." Sally wrapped her in a hug, ignoring Arthur's pointed stare. Tessa could feel him watching her and knew he wanted a decision sooner rather than later so he could come up with a plan. But she couldn't give him an answer until she knew for certain and every passing hour made it feel less likely that Landon was coming.

"Random question." Tessa blinked back her tears and tried to focus on something she could control. "Would you by chance have some extra mason jars? I'd like to use up the chicken and veggies in the freezer in a big pot of soup and can the leftovers. I can give you half of whatever it makes."

Despite her protests, Sally insisted she would watch the kids while Tessa ran back home to gather the ingredients. She glanced over her shoulder one more time before rushing into the house. *They'll be okay for a few minutes without me.* Rationally, she knew this. But some primitive urge forced her to hurry anyway. The whole world seemed too quiet without them.

Moose followed her around the house as she grabbed the dented crab boil pot and opened the deep freezer. Five days and everything was defrosted, the chest barely holding the temperature at 45 degrees. It was 40 degrees this morning. At least the last of it wouldn't go to waste.

The ten-pound bag of chicken thigh meat and five-pound bag of chicken breasts went into the pot and she piled the rest of the bags of veggies on top. She'd worry about sorting the ingredients later once she got back across the street. In the kitchen, she stopped for bullion powder and spices. Moose settled onto the rug and waited for her to start cooking.

"I promise I'll bring you some back." Tessa lifted the heavy pot onto her hip as she kicked the pantry door closed and grabbed a bucket of water.

"That was fast." Sally laughed when Tessa came into the kitchen. "I figured you'd enjoy the break. How long has it been since you had one?"

"Six months." She lifted the pot onto the counter and glanced outside. Emily was tugging Arthur by his arm, begging him to push her on the tire swing. "Oh no. He doesn't have to play with her. She can be such a little boss. I'll tell her to leave him alone."

Sally stopped her from opening the door. "Arthur is fine. He may look like a crusty old man, but he's really a big kid at heart. Let him play again for a little bit."

Tessa stood back and watched them. A wide grin lit up Arthur's serious face as he twisted the tire in circles to tighten the rope. Mason and Emily sat nestled inside, clinging to the rubber sides, and their squeals turned to happy screams when he released it to let them spin. Sally stood next to Tessa smiling even as tears pooled in the corners of her eyes.

Tessa reached for the woman's hand. "I'm sure Anissa will be okay and find her way back home soon."

"Me too." Sally nodded. "Now let's get started on this soup."

It was odd working in someone else's kitchen, but they found an easy rhythm. The evening faded away in a humid fog of chicken broth and steam from the pressure cooker. Sally made cornbread in the cast iron skillet and cooked it on the grill. They shared dinner while they waited for the jars to seal. By the end of the night, they were able to fill eighteen quart size jars and although Sally tried to put her foot down, Tessa only took nine.

"At least let Arthur help you carry them home," Sally said with a sigh.

"I've got it. Thank you though. And I'll bring you the jars back when we are done with them. Mason, grab the water bucket."

Arthur took the heavy pot from her hands before she even made it out the door. He ignored her protest and started walking as the sun set on their little hill. Emily and Mason raced to the house with the bucket dragging along the road.

"I really can carry that," Tessa muttered. "You guys have already done too much."

"I know that you can carry it." Arthur set the pot down on her front porch. When he bent over, his gun holster stuck out from under his shirt. The sight of it made Tessa feel awful. She'd left her gun in the safe as if the real terrors could only happen at night and here he was always carrying a weapon and now carrying his jars for her.

Her cheeks flushed, but she tried to be polite. "Thank you again, for everything."

"Yep." He nodded.

"Listen. I know you want an answer on if I'm staying or going so you can plan for what happens next, but I don't know if I can stay here without Landon. Our only family is up in Idaho and we would all be safer there. I'm serious that you should come with me."

Arthur was silent, staring at his house. Just when she thought he was about to leave, he turned to look at her. "If things were different, I'd agree with you. But we can't leave right now. Don't let that stop you from making your decision though. Either way, you'll still have options."

"Either way?" Her forehead creased as she stood waiting for an explanation.

"Mommy!" Emily screamed from inside the house. "Mason took my doll and won't give it back."

"I did not!"

Arthur chuckled, but a deep sadness filled his eyes. "We'll talk later. Go take care of your kids."

"Your marshmallow is burning."

"I like them burnt."

Tessa's eyes fluttered open and she groaned, trying to hold to the image of Landon's face smiling at her over the campfire within her dreams. The smell of wood smoke was still in the air trapping her between the unconscious and reality. Gray morning light filtered through the window. Mason's too big feet pressed against her back as he pushed himself up against the pillow and yawned.

Please don't wake up. Her brain began to clear. *It can't be morning yet. I swear I just fell asleep.*

She inhaled deeply as she came fully awake. There were a lot of decisions that had to be made today. The taste of smoke filled her lungs. Her eyes shot open and she scrambled out of bed.

Something was on fire but the smoke alarms weren't screaming. *Do the alarms work without power?* She raced to the kitchen and checked the range, then ran outside but the grill sat covered in the shadows from the early gray dawn.

Backtracking, she searched the house for clues as to where the smoke was coming from. Her heart sank as she threw open the front door. Behind Sally and Arthur's house, above the mountains to the south, an orange glow topped the peaks and black smoke settled above it. She coughed, inhaling the putrid air as she stepped bare foot outside. The smoke drifted over the valley below like a muted fog.

And on the horizon in the distance, thick gray clouds billowed above the mountains to the east where another fire was starting. Within the smoke was the rising sun burning red and angry. She ran back inside the house and slammed the door a little too hard as if blocking out the world could slow down time.

Fires are common in Southern California. Don't panic. Except… Whatever guilt she had last night about needing to leave when Sally wanted her to stay was being replaced by a heavy fear. If she didn't go soon, would she even be able to make it over the mountains?

"I smell smoke." Mason was suddenly right beside her and Tessa screamed, jumping out of her skin. His gap-toothed grin widened as he laughed.

"You scared the crap out of me." She pressed her hand over her heart, willing it to stop racing. "There's a fire over the mountains, but it's not close to us."

"Like the fire when we moved here last summer?" Mason walked to the kitchen and pulled the refrigerator door open out of habit, frowning when the dark shelves with warm condiments stared back at him.

"Something like that." Except last summer there were working vehicles, firetrucks racing down the freeways to join the fight and airplanes flying overhead to drop retardant on the flames. Now there was no noise. No one was coming. She closed her eyes and breathed deeply, the smoke in the air burning her chapped lips.

"We're out of milk." Mason closed the refrigerator door.

"I know," Tessa whispered.

Smoke seeped its way into every moment of the morning routine and her anxiety grew with each breath she took. It was another taunting reminder of how powerless humans really were when the elements had their way. But she couldn't close her eyes and pretend all of this wasn't real anymore.

Mason finished the math problems she'd scribbled on a piece of spiral notebook paper and held it up for her to inspect.

"Perfect." She ruffled his messy brown hair.

"Is mine?" Emily stood with her chest puffed out, shoving the drawing she'd meticulously worked on into Tessa's face. She took a step back to see.

Stick figure Emily stood holding stick figure Mason's hand next to an oversize stick figure Tessa with a mass of curling red lines on top of her head. Moose sat beside them with triangles for ears and a bright pink tongue. The four of them posed by a box shaped replica of Old Blue. And in the corner of the page, as far away from them as it could get, was a stick figure daddy with short spiky brown hair and the biggest turned C for a smile.

"It's beautiful." Tessa's eyes filled with tears as she held the page in her hand and Emily skipped to the living room. She focused on stick Landon and wished he was a little bit closer, enough so he didn't seem so out of reach, and stick Tessa could hold his hand too. Drops of tears fell onto the page and she tried to smear them off with her thumb.

The knock at the door made her heart stop.

"It's Daddy!" Emily screamed, sending toys skidding across the tile as she and Moose flew toward the entryway.

"Don't open that door," Tessa cried as she scanned the room looking for a weapon. The pistol was still locked away upstairs.

"Mom?" Mason stood an arm's length away and looked to her in confusion. She shoved him behind her back and grabbed Emily by her arm.

"You're hurting me." Emily tried to yank her elbow free.

"Stop." The fear in Tessa's voice was enough to silence them both. Moose's bark echoed through the house as the knock sounded again.

"Temecula City Police."

"It's the cops," Mason said, worry etched on his face.

"I know." Tessa clutched her stomach and tried not to throw up. "Go to the back patio. If anything happens, take Emily and run. Don't stop until you get to Sally's house."

"What's going to happen, Mommy?" Emily's voice cracked as her eyes opened wide in fear.

"Nothing." She kissed the top of her head and put the girl's hand in her brother's hand. "Just go."

They found the body. Tessa's heart slammed in her chest and her feet dragged as she made her way to the door. *I'm going to jail and there is no one to take care of my kids. I shouldn't have listened to Arthur. I should have reported it.* The fist beat on the door again. *Oh God, what do I do?*

"Good morning, ma'am." Officer O'Brien stood on her porch steps with his hand on his belt. His sun glasses were gone and his face was more haggard than it was a few days ago.

"Morning." Her throat was dry.

"Sorry to bother you, but I was wondering if we could talk for a minute."

Tessa leaned her head out far enough to check the road. His police cruiser sat parked in her driveway but his partner wasn't in it. *Would he come to arrest me alone?* She pulled her head back inside. "What's this about?"

Officer O'Brien gave her a disarming smile. She'd seen that face on the deputies who worked with her dad when she was growing up. He was either playing the good cop angle, or he wanted something from her. Neither scenario made her comfortable.

"I heard something yesterday from one of your neighbors and I figured it was best to verify it with you."

162

"My neighbors?" *Would Arthur have said something to him?* It must have been someone from down the hill. Someone who heard the gunshots the other night.

"Well, I guess they aren't your neighbors anymore." He scratched the stubble on his chin. "A young couple with a newborn baby came to the shelter Tuesday afternoon when they ran out of formula. We asked them about working vehicles and they mentioned seeing you drive a truck the day prior."

"That's what this is about?" Tessa's jaw dropped. It couldn't have been Olivia or Charlie, they weren't what she'd call young, but all the other closed curtains in the subdivision. Spying through windows because there wasn't anything else to do. Did her neighbors tell the cops about her?

"Would it be about something else?" His smile briefly faltered.

"I figured it was more bad news." She regained her composure, forcing a disinterested sigh. "Did I break the law somehow by driving my truck?"

"No." He studied her face a moment longer before deciding to let it go. "But when I came here earlier this week, you told me you didn't have a working vehicle."

"My husband fixed it." She hoped he couldn't hear the nervousness behind the lie.

His eyes widened with a frantic urgency. "Can I speak with him?"

"I'm sorry." Every muscle in her body tensed. "He's not home right now."

"When will he be back?"

"I don't know." The harsh truth of the statement caught her off guard and she choked back a sob. Officer O'Brien took a step back.

"So, is he here or not?"

Tessa bit her lip, trying not to cry. "He'll be home soon. I just don't know when."

"Listen." He sighed. "I've got almost three thousand people already spread out in four different shelters. Elderly people, kids, most of them with some kind of disability. The hospital is working limited hours with the generators, but trying to get these people medical care is a logistical nightmare. We've got maybe thirty volunteers with working vehicles. There were more in the beginning, but the longer this thing goes on, less of them show up. I'm kind of at my wits end here. Every day locals and refugees are coming in from the freeway needing some kind of assistance. With the fires down south, this is only going to get worse. If you could help us out, I'd really appreciate it."

In another life, she wouldn't have hesitated. But she didn't have the option now. "I've got kids. I can't put us in a situation where they wouldn't be safe."

Officer O'Brien folded his arms over his chest. The words he wanted to say were stuck in his throat, but she could hear them anyway. Civic duty. Taking care of your neighbors. But the dangers were too great. The truck was her only means of escape. She couldn't just hand it over and she couldn't risk taking the kids with her to run errands for this cop.

"Maybe you could discuss this with your husband when he gets home," Officer O'Brien broke the tense silence.

"I'll do that," she said.

The officer shook his head as he turned to leave. "Thank you for your time." The statement seemed so common place that it felt wrong in this situation. A cold thought sliced its way through her core. *How much time do I have?*

"How long until you come take my truck?"

His shoulders stiffened, but he didn't turn around. "Let's hope it doesn't come to that."

Tessa watched him drive down the hill. Smoke filled the sky and the blood red sun backdropped his retreating police car. When he was out of sight, she forced herself to breathe normally again and step back inside the house.

"Mason. Emily. Get your shoes on."

Moose lifted his head from the couch, waiting to see if he was invited this time.

"You too boy." She reached for his collar. "I need you to keep an eye on them."

"Sorry to bother you again," Tessa said as Sally opened the screen door.

"Nonsense." The woman smiled. "You three are never a bother. Or should I say you four." Sally laughed as Moose's bushy tail almost knocked her over and he gave her hand a sloppy lick. "What are you all up to today?"

"Why don't you three go play outside?" Tessa motioned for the kids to leave and they dragged Moose along with them. "Is Arthur here?"

"I'm here." Arthur pushed open the cellar door. He wiped the sweat from his forehead before replacing his cap and looking to her with tired eyes. Sally moved to his side, reaching for his hand as she leaned against him for support.

"What happened?" Tessa searched their faces, hoping this had nothing to do with their daughter.

"We haven't been able to reach a friend of ours in a few days. He's up near L.A. and Arthur is worried about him," Sally explained.

"He'll be fine," Arthur grumbled, but he didn't look convinced.

It probably wasn't the right time, but this revelation only added to her sense of urgency. "The cop who was here the other day came back. One of the people who live in the subdivision told him my truck still works. He's asking for help because it seems like the shelters are filling up."

"That's good to know." Arthur nodded. "Thank you for the warning."

"What warning?" Tessa gasped as her anxiety began to grow. "I'm telling you that if they find out we shot someone, he can arrest me and confiscate my property. I can't go to jail. There's no one to take care of my kids. I need to do something. I need to bury the body."

"Take a breath." Arthur chuckled, even though nothing about this was funny. "I already took care of the bodies. I didn't want a mess of coyotes poking their noses around here. And no one is going to arrest you. I was the one who shot them. If they decide there needs to be justice for two dead tweakers, I'll be the one taking the blame."

Her shoulders sagged as the weight fell from them. It had only been a week but she was already trusting these people with her life. She felt guilty for not meeting them sooner.

But they weren't Landon. Time was moving too fast and too many things were happening at once. She wasn't stupid enough to wait until it all spiraled out of control. She had to go, with or without him.

"Would you guys mind watching the kids for a few hours? There's something I need to do."

"You have your gun?" Arthur stood on the front porch while Sally pulled out dusty board games for the kids. Moose had already made himself at home and was snoring on the faded green carpet in front of the sofa.

"I'm going to run back to the house and get it before I go, but I don't think they'll let me on base with it." Her gaze traveled to the holster that was hidden under his baggy shirt. She needed one of those.

"Keep it in the truck if you have to," he said. "And what's your plan when you get there?"

"I'm going to try the back gate this time. It's a longer drive, but I can avoid the freeways and main roads altogether. Hopefully they won't have it closed off or there won't be as many people if they do, but they'll have to have someone standing guard and maybe they'll have some information about the guys on deployment."

"Are you sure you want to do this? He'd make his way home if he was here and they might not have the intel you are hoping for." Arthur tried to give her an out.

She nodded, wiping her sweaty palms on the back of her jeans. "I can't sit here waiting anymore and I can't leave without trying to find out where he is at least one more time."

Tessa glared at the cookie cutter houses in the subdivision as she drove past them, daring someone to report this trip to the cops, and then turned on the worn road up the mountain that would lead her deeper into the hills. It was slow going up the switchbacks, but she wasn't about to break the 30mph speed limit. The road was empty except for a broken down convertible up ahead that had conveniently decided to stop in both lanes. Her stomach flipped as she had to ease two tires off the edge of the cliff with no guardrail to stop her descent if the truck rolled down the mountain face.

She breathed a sigh of relief when she made it to the road that cut through the mountain instead. Southern California mansions lined either side, tucked away from the eyesore of the valley below with looming gates that didn't allow anyone in. She pressed hard on the gas pedal to make up for lost time and flew down the open road. Every mile she drove away from her kids felt like a mistake, but she had to do this for them too. *They'll be okay.*

An outcropping of trailers dotted the foothills that sat below the mountaintop. Tessa rode the brakes down the incline until she was on the backroad leading to the small town of Fallbrook. There was a group of people in the dirt parking lot of the trailer park to her right. Kids tumbled around on the ground and a baby with a sagging diaper cried for its mother's arms. The adults watched the truck speed by with interest, moving closer to the wire fence as she passed, but she didn't slow down until she was forced to drive around the abandoned Honda Prius to get into the Albertson's parking lot.

The grocery store windows were busted out, the glass shattered over the asphalt reflecting in the sun like diamonds. Empty shelves were knocked over and came spilling from the building onto the sidewalk. Tessa craned her neck looking for police or whoever did this, but no one was out walking around. The other businesses in the shopping center that weren't boarded up had all suffered the same fate as the grocery store.

She hesitated with her foot on the brake. Just around the back of the store was a quarter mile road to the gate. Normally she'd drive up without hesitation, show her ID card, and be let in. But if the situation was the same as the main gate, she didn't want to plow into a group of people with no way to turn around.

Guess I'm walking. She backed into an empty parking space and killed the engine. Her hands shook as she tucked the stupid pink pistol into the waistband of her jeans. She was only going to get a closer look, see what was coming before she dove headfirst into it, but she glanced over her shoulder to make sure no one was watching and popped the hood to Old Blue to disconnect the battery just in case.

The smoke was worse up here and it burned her eyes as she jogged across the broken glass that crunched under her worn sneakers. She kept herself pressed against the side of the building, staying in the shadows until she had no choice but to leave the safety of the structure and dash across the alley. Her fingers twitched, reaching for one of her children out of instinct and a moment of panic made her heart flutter. *They're safe. You'll be right back.*

The squeaking wheel of a broken grocery cart sounded from her right. She ran for the cover of the green dumpster up ahead. An old man with leather skin and only a few whisps of white greasy hair on his balding head pushed the metal cart filled with trash

170

bags out of the alley. He looked at her with hollow eyes, working his toothless jaw but saying nothing as he continued forward. Tessa watched him go and felt whatever hope she had slip further out of reach.

Not again. Outside the gate it was as if a tent city had sprung up in the middle of the road. Dozens of bodies pressed together in the sticky heat under tarps and ripped up tents left wide open to catch the slightest breeze. Beyond them, the gate was barricaded off. But a uniformed Marine was on the other side of the fence, patrolling the line and watching the crowd. *If I can just talk to him.* She took a step forward, leaving the safety of the dumpster without a plan.

A rough hand grabbed her elbow and pulled her toward the unwashed face of a man with bad breath and a gold chain on his chest. His beady eyes stared straight into hers. "You got an ID card?" he hissed.

"Get off of me." Tessa shoved him back. His grip tightened on her arm as she glanced to the gate. They were within earshot, if she screamed the guard would hear it.

The man knew it too and twisted her around, slamming his meaty palm over her mouth and pressing her back against his chest. "We're going somewhere to talk. Don't make a scene."

Tessa chomped her teeth into his flesh and threw her head backwards. The sickening sound of crunching bone reverberated through her head as his nose crushed against her skull.

"Don't touch me," Tessa screamed, fumbling for the pistol as the thug staggered back.

He raised his hands in the air, looking past her to the gate, while blood poured down his face. "I didn't mean any harm." Her fingers connected with the frame of the pistol just as the man took off running down the alley like a rat.

She let it go and pulled down her shirt to cover it, holding her arms over her chest and sucking in shaky breaths. *This is a mistake.* But the gate was less than a hundred yards away. She moved forward slowly; her eyes wide as she watched every person on the street with a hawk like intensity. Her kids needed her to come back home. She wouldn't be caught off guard again.

Each step she took, she scanned her surroundings watching for someone to come out from the makeshift shelters. She assessed their clothes, their body movements, and stole glances over her shoulder to make sure no one was coming at her from behind. Dirty faces watched her back, disinterested like they'd been seeing the same scene for a while and nothing could surprise them anymore. But despite the smell of trash and sweat, not all of them looked homeless.

A young woman clutched a Coach purse to her chest as she sat in the shade staring despondently at the gate. Well fed children clung to a woman's floral dress. Aging men with button down shirts and veterans' caps on their heads gathered together with Styrofoam cups over a Coleman grill and a pot of

172

coffee. Closer to the gate was a group of people hopelessly waving their ID cards in the air. Tessa avoided that crowd and slipped behind the brick wall with the "Don't Drink and Drive" sign tacked to the mortar.

She stumbled through the brush coated with remnants of plastic bags and waterlogged paper under the palm trees, working her way to the chain link fence where the guard was sure to patrol. Every sense was heightened as she scanned the overgrown lot waiting for someone to attack. Her heart beat faster at every snap of a twig. The weight of the pistol was reassuring, but she didn't dare pull it out yet. Not when she was so close to getting an answer.

She laced her fingers through the fence and the cold metal instantly enraged her. This stupid thin wall, the military base behind it, the thing that took away her husband and wasn't giving him back even as the whole world fell apart. It was all right here behind a chain link fence and there was nothing she could do about it.

"Someone tell me where HM2 Ward is." She grabbed the fence and shook it as hard as she could, feeling the metal vibrate down the line with the force of her pain. Every moment spent waiting, every heart-breaking move, holidays and birthdays missed, all the tears her children had cried, and every fear that was bottled up from these past few days and the years before it burned like a gaping wound as she screamed, "I want him back!"

She could feel herself losing it; control, sanity, her voice as it tore out her throat. They were going to rush her with weapons drawn, force her to her knees in the dirt. She knew it, but she didn't care. As long as they told her something in the end.

"It's not worth it," a woman's voice spoke from somewhere to the right. Tessa spun around, her hand already on the pistol. "I screamed until my voice was raw and they couldn't tell me anything more. When the sun sets, they'll send out their next humanitarian push. It's better to ask your questions then."

"Where are you?" Tessa stepped back from the fence as her eyes darted around the overgrown stretch of weeds and trees. She wasn't careful enough. *I don't think I'm strong enough for this.* She forced away the self-doubt and held the pistol in her hands as she tried to pinpoint where the voice was coming from.

"You can shoot me if you want." The voice was barely a whisper. Tessa turned to the side, her gun trained on the palm tree shedding its bark and the shadow it cast on the ground. The woman peeked around the tree trunk with big brown sunglasses hiding her eyes. She gathered her trench coat around her and sighed. "I'm not sure I'm surviving this anyway."

"Surviving what?" Tessa lowered the pistol a fraction of an inch.

"The end of the world as we know it," the woman almost hummed the words. *Okay. She's weird.* But the woman didn't seem like a threat.

Still, she didn't put away the gun. "What were you saying about humanitarian pushes?"

"They move a unit out at sunset and sunrise to distribute bottled water and some food to the people hanging around outside the gate. I walked here and made it too late last night, but they were out first thing in the morning like I was told."

"Is it just for the locals? Are they letting anyone in?" Tessa spoke too fast, needing to know every detail of what was happening.

"It's for everyone." The woman shrank back against the tree, hiding her body in the shade again. "I mean, they aren't requiring IDs for the aid they are handing out if that's what you're asking. They are keeping a running tally of who's outside, but only sponsors, you know, active duty, are being escorted through the gates. Dependent IDs, Veteran IDs, they're all being told to wait unless they have a sponsor with them."

Tessa touched the wallet in her front pocket. She was only a wife, *a dependent*, and that's what her ID card said. Her husband's career was his own and she never had a problem with that, right until the moment where the supposedly family friendly military would deny her entry onto base if he wasn't with her.

She took a step back and tucked her pistol into her waistband, glancing at the gate and the world that was hidden behind it. All of this was a mistake. She needed to get back home to her kids. "Do you know by chance if the USS McKinley made it home from deployment?"

"You too, huh?" The woman's voice cracked as she started to cry. "They are saying it hasn't and they haven't been in contact with any ships. No one has any word on returning troops or if they're even coming back at all."

She knew it was coming and had braced herself for the possibility, but it still sank like a heavy stone in the pit of her stomach. Landon wasn't coming home. She had her answer. It was time to leave. The woman's soft cries kept her rooted to the spot. "Was your husband on the McKinley too?"

"My fiancé," the woman laughed bitterly. "I don't even have an ID card. I don't belong here."

"I don't either." Tessa turned to go. Something held her back. She knew it was dumb, her kids needed her to hurry, but her heart was stronger than her head. "Do you need help getting somewhere? You said you walked here last night."

"I'll be fine." The words were so defeated and broken that Tessa stepped closer, her hands outstretched as if approaching a wounded bird.

Sunlight filtered through the palm leaves and smoke above, reflecting off her brown sunglasses and highlighting the purple bruising on her left cheekbone. Her soft blond hair was cut in a straight angle that pointed to the woman's bandaged chin.

"Who did this to you?" Tessa gasped.

"Some jerks that came through my apartment complex." Her split bottom lip began to quiver. "I'm okay."

"Like hell you are." Tessa extended her hand to help her up. "Come on. We need to get you out of here."

The woman hesitated, looking at Tessa's outstretched fingers, and she shrank down against the tree. "I don't need your pity."

"It isn't pity." Tessa wasn't in the mood to play around. Her kids were waiting for her and she had to finish packing. "I have a truck and can take you wherever you need to go, but I don't have time to waste. You need to get up."

The woman pressed herself against the tree, using it for support as she stretched out her legs. Loose gray sweatpants were cinched tightly at the waist and she wore a tank top under the brown trench coat that fell just below her knees. The clothes were a strange choice in the Southern California heat, almost designed to be as ugly as possible. When the woman stood, she was at least a foot taller than Tessa. The clothes. The height. Something clicked.

"Wait. I've seen you before." Except the woman wasn't dressed like this at all the last time she'd seen her. She had on a navy-blue pencil skirt and white heels that showcased her long and killer legs. Tessa remembered staring at her, feeling jealous and insecure in her simple sundress stained by Emily's fruit punch juice box.

"At the tarmac the day the guys left. You're the wife of Gunnery Sergeant Fu… Fi… Fu-Man… Fuyo." Tessa cringed in embarrassment. "Look, I'm really awful with names but that one just isn't fair."

"Fuimaono." A smile spread across her face and she winced, touching her bottom lip. "And I'm just the fiancé, remember. It's nice to meet you. My name's Robin."

"Tessa." She shook her hand. A week ago, this would have seemed impossible, standing outside the fence of base in the trash filled weeds with a gunnery sergeant's fiancé. But apparently a lot can happen in a week and she wasn't going to stick around to find out how much worse it could get. "We need to get out of here. Where do you live? I'll give you a ride back home."

12
Landon

"Are comms still down?" Sgt. Sierra asked when Landon stepped behind him in the chow line.

"I'm going to check after I get something to eat." Landon twisted the ring on his finger. He'd slept in this morning instead of heading to the computer. It was hard to break away from his dreams when they were of her and the kids. At least the ship was moving again.

"Half rations," Sgt. Sierra grimaced as he grabbed his tray.

"They could feed me dog food for all I care right now." Landon carried his breakfast over to the empty table and sat down on the attached swivel stool. A cup of rice, brown gravy with chunks of what must be meat, and a half slice of cold white bread stared back at him. He barely tasted it in his haste to get something into his stomach.

"You want mine too?" Sgt. Sierra asked with his eyebrow raised.

"I'm good." Landon mopped up what was left of the gravy with the bread. "That might have actually been dog food." Sgt. Sierra ripped open a stack of sugar packets and poured the granules into his coffee.

"You're going to get diabetes." Landon grimaced when he reached for another sugar pack.

"What are you my doctor or something?" Sgt. Sierra sipped the coffee flavored sugar and sighed.

"That's exactly what I am." Landon downed the rest of his black coffee and tossed the empty plastic mug on the tray.

"Alright Doc." He rolled his eyes. "What do you got going on today?"

"Wellness checks on every single one of you window lickers after I go check on Martinez. He should be getting released from his 72-hour confinement soon."

"About Martinez…" Sgt. Sierra's voice trailed off as he looked around the mess deck. Satisfied no one was listening, he leaned forward on the table. "Are you doing okay with all that?"

"Why wouldn't I be?" Landon folded his arms over his chest.

"Look, I'm not trying to pry open old wounds or anything, but the way you acted the other day reminded me of Campbell and I wanted to make sure you're alright."

Landon's eyes darkened when he heard the name and he closed them to block out the too bright fluorescent light. "That was a different situation."

"I know that. It's just the way you lost it for a minute put me right back there."

"You really think now is the best time to bring this up?" Landon opened his eyes and stared at him, seeing the kid he once was with his face streaked in blood and dirt as he dragged him away from Campbell's dead body and merging it with the version of his friend who sat before him now. "Campbell didn't want to die. Martinez is a different story."

"I know." Sgt. Sierra lowered his face. "But you beat yourself up for the rest of that deployment about not carrying him out of there fast enough and I know how that shit lingers. Campbell, Martinez, none of them are your fault."

"Maybe you should've joined the Navy if you wanted to be a shrink." Landon chuckled.

"I'm serious, man. Let it out if you need to."

Landon shook his head. "Thanks, but no thanks. Do you remember Campbell though? That kid was a good dude."

"Yeah, he was. Didn't he sneak in that bottle of Jägermeister into the barracks and get us all drunk in Yuma?" Sgt. Sierra studied Landon's expression, waiting to see if he needed to keep talking.

"Yep." Landon nodded and looked away.

"You know I probably wouldn't be here if it weren't for you and I know a few other guys that feel the same." Sgt. Sierra choked out the words he hoped would help ease the guilt Landon carried.

Landon forced himself to smile. "I wouldn't be here if it weren't for you either."

Sgt. Sierra put his hands under his chin and puckered his lips as he batted his long dark lashes flirtatiously. "Are you going to kiss me now?"

"I've got something you can kiss." Landon laughed as he grabbed his tray and walked away.

He didn't want to think about the past as he walked alone to medical trying to get to a computer before the day began and he didn't want to think about what the future might be like either. The last few days had slipped by in a blur of rumors and meaningless nothing work to fill the time. Brooms to push, random training to attend, meals that weren't filling enough.

But he was getting closer and that had to count for something. The ship was speeding through the pacific waters. Soon he'd be home and all the anxious rumors could be laid to rest. It didn't matter what was going to happen, he was going to hold his wife again. Not even the sun could take that away.

"What are you doing here, HM2?" Chief Elyse's sharp voice cut through the medical office.

"Morning Chief." Landon nodded, hoping today was not the day she chose to unleash her fury at him. "I want to try and send an email out before I start working."

"Don't bother," Chief Elyse said as she powered down the computer. There were tears in her eyes reflecting the bluish glow of the screen before it turned off.

"Comms are still down?" Landon asked, his hope for a good day quickly fading. Tessa must be worried sick by now. He really wanted to explain to her about the delay and see if she'd written anything else besides that awful last email he couldn't stop thinking about.

"Of course they're still down." She put her head in her hands and breathed deeply through her nose. In the short time he'd known her, she'd been angry, vindictive, snarky, but never outwardly emotional like this.

Landon took a step back. "Are you doing alright, Chief?"

She looked up at him with her signature glare. "Did I ask for your concern, Ward? No. Now get out of here." Every rational part of him wanted to run. He'd try to email Tessa later when he got another break.

But he hesitated. *Sierra must have got under my skin.* "No disrespect, Chief, but I'm serious. Are you okay?"

Chief Elyse rubbed her fingers under her eyes to clear the tears and checked the tightly wound bun at the nape of her neck to make sure no hairs were out of place. In an instant, her collected mask slipped back on as if the outburst never happened. She seemed to weigh her options, giving Landon a cold look over and the quiet room was filled with uncomfortable silence.

"Alright then." Landon nodded as he took another step back. There was only one other short woman her size who scared him as much as the chief did, but Tessa's love made up for her temper. Chief Elyse had no love to give.

"Wait, HM2." Chief Elyse sighed. "I'm fine. My parents have temporary custody of my son for this deployment because I couldn't secure a local caregiver. They were supposed to fly out today after my mom's cataract surgery to meet me in California, but I wasn't able to wire them money for the tickets because all the systems are down."

"That sucks, Chief." It was strange having a real conversation with her, like she was somehow becoming a real person despite being a chief. He felt bad for her. He really did.

"Yes HM2." She narrowed her eyes, her fingernails clicking against the desktop. "It really does suck."

"But hey," Landon backtracked as he realized his poor choice of words, "they say were making great time. I've never made it back in less than six days from Hawaii, but rumors are we'll be there tomorrow. We should be close to shore soon. Maybe you can get cell service."

"Maybe." She looked away, but Landon caught the flash of fear in her eyes. His jaw tensed and he refused to acknowledge that same fear.

"It won't be as bad as they're all saying. The government will have safeguards in place for a massive solar storm. It's not like they'd just ignore that burning ball of fire in the sky and pretend it won't ever affect us. I'm sure everything will be okay."

"Do you really think that?" Chief Elyse whispered.

Did he? He had no other choice but to believe it was true until he could do something about it. If his family was suffering…

Landon gave a short nod. "Yes. I do."

The wheels of the stool skid across the deck, squeaking as Chief Elyse pushed herself away from the table. "Well, then you're dumber than you look."

Landon waited to leave the office until he was sure Chief Elyse was gone from the medical bay and then pulled the stool over to the patient bed. "Hey, brother. How are you feeling?"

LCpl Martinez groaned as he rolled over and offered a small smile. "Better. My brain isn't racing so much. I can't wait to get out of here though. It's almost too quiet if you know what I mean."

"Don't say that." Landon tilted back Martinez's head to check the bruising on his neck. There wasn't much. He'd literally caught him just in time.

"Say what?" His pupils were dilated but that was probably from the meds.

"It's a medical thing. Never say it's too quiet in a hospital."

"My bad." LCpl Martinez chuckled. "So, are they still letting me out today?"

"Commander Jenkins will give the final say tonight but they should be." Landon pulled over the vitals machine and wrapped the cuff around

Martinez's arm. The device whirred to life and pumped air through the tube.

"You're looking good." Landon pulled at the Velcro on the cuff. Blood pressure 110/79. Pulse at 62 beats per minute. "The meds making you feel relaxed?"

"Yeah." Martinez nodded. "I feel like I could sleep for another week."

Landon made a mental note to ask the commander to lower the dosage before they discharged him. "Alright man, is there anything else you need me to bring you before they let you out?"

"Nah. I think I'm good." Martinez rested his head on the starch white pillow and closed his eyes. Landon watched the even rise and fall of his chest a minute longer before turning on his heel to leave.

"Hey Doc," Martinez called out. "What's going to happen when we get back?"

Landon sighed, taking a seat on the stool again. "You're going to get better. You'll learn to deal with the stuff inside your head and we'll make sure to get you the right treatment. I'll put you on limited duty for a while. Things won't be as stressful while we get you sorted out and you'll get to see your wife and newborn child."

"That's not what I meant. Do you think the rumors are true? What if the home we are going back to isn't home at all?" Martinez spoke with his eyes still closed.

Landon chose his next words carefully. "Do you think these thoughts are helping or hurting you right now?"

"Neither." He shrugged. "I'm just thinking them out loud to the universe. But I can't stop wondering if my wife is okay."

Landon rested his elbows on his knees and sighed, wanting to be somewhere else where he wasn't having this conversation. "You live on base, right? They'll take care of everyone if there is some kind of emergency. She'll be alright. All of our families will."

"You're right, Doc." LCpl Martinez yawned, his voice dreamy and distant as he fell asleep.

Am I? Landon could feel his blood pressure rising as he stood in the passageway outside of medical. It was all too much. Sgt. Sierra shouldn't have brought up Campbell this morning. Chief crying, the fear on her face. Martinez's drugged up concern for his wife. *I just want to send a damn email.* The walls he'd built to maintain calm in chaos over the years were starting to crumble. He moved his thumb to his ring and the tiniest crack formed in the silicone band disrupting the familiar comfort of the spin. His chest tightened and he clutched his hand in a fist.

Landon ducked into the berthing and changed into PT gear, hurrying so he didn't run into Sierra or anyone else that needed him right now. He grabbed his phone and shoved the earbuds in as he walked the corridors to the gym. His thoughts raced and he tried to calm himself with plans of what he was going to do when he got home. There were family trips he wanted to take. Mason still wasn't riding his bike all that well according to the email Tessa had sent before the last one and he intended to fix that.

But the rumors of how bad this solar storm thing could be wouldn't leave him alone. Were Tessa and the kids alright? *They have to be.* Landon's jaw was clenched as he walked into the gym. A few people were milling about the machines but the treadmills were abandoned. He jumped on the track and cranked up the volume off his phone. *Don't think. Run.*

He beat himself up with every painful minute, forcing his legs to work harder. His lungs burned as he struggled to breathe but still, he kept running. Every time he saw her face in his mind, he increased the incline and the speed. But he didn't stop even as sweat poured down his back and his muscles screamed in protest. *She will be okay.* Something deep in his gut told him to move faster. *If the world was falling apart… If the rumors were true… If…If…*

His heart tried to launch itself from his chest. A hand reached out and hit the red stop button long before Landon was ready to slow down.

"What the hell?" He yanked the earbuds from his ears and adrenaline coursed through his veins as he turned to see GySgt. Fuimaono standing there.

The track slowed and Landon grabbed the handholds for support as he gasped for air. "Why'd you do that, Gunny?"

GySgt. Fuimaono arched an eyebrow, looking him over with a frown. "You've been at this for over an hour. I think you need to breathe."

Landon's legs felt weak and he put his arms above his head. The muted notes of the heavy metal song came drifting from his fallen earbuds as he walked a few steps. *Everything is going to be okay.*

GySgt. Fuimaono moved to the bench and positioned himself under the chest press bar racked out with three stacks of 45lb weights on each side, grunting as he lifted it free from the holds. The Samoan warrior glanced back at Landon with mild curiosity and shook his head. "Don't you have patients to see or something?"

13
Tessa

"Crap." Tessa let out a low breath as she stepped onto the parking lot. A group of people were walking toward them from across the street. Some of the faces she remembered from the trailer park a few miles back and one of them was pointing at the truck.

She broke into a full sprint, sliding across the broken glass and unlocked Old Blue to pop the hood. Her eyes never left the group as she tightened the loose screw on the positive battery terminal.

"Hey, wait a minute," a woman from the group called out.

Robin slid into the cab of the truck. The color was drained from her face as she slammed the passenger door closed. "I think we should get out of here now."

"Working on it." The engine roared to life and the tires kicked up bits of debris as she accelerated onto the road.

"My apartment is down in Escondido." Robin was shaking and she put her hands under her legs as she turned to stare out the back window.

Tessa almost hit the brakes. "Escondido? You walked here from there?"

"I hike a lot." Robin shrugged. Warning bells rang in Tessa's head as she turned onto the main street. Escondido was the complete opposite direction from home and a heck of a lot more populated. She'd been there once to take Emily to the Build A Bear workshop in the massive mall.

Tessa glanced at Robin from the corner of her eye. Sure, she'd given her word, but she might have bit off more than she could chew. "Are you positive you want to go home?"

Robin leaned back against the seat and blew out a heavy breath that moved the hair off her sunglasses. "Where else is there to go?"

Tension knotted the muscles of her shoulders and neck as Tessa clung to the steering wheel. The red dial showed a quarter tank left. There was just enough to get Robin to her apartment and get back home. The gas can was still in the garage. Landon had filled it before he left. The ache of missing him hit her hard.

Thick pine trees lined old highway 395 until the boulders and rocks gave way to clear parcels of open land. The industrial buildings loomed in the distance, flat topped and abandoned. A few days ago, she'd driven this stretch of road, but it already felt like a lifetime since.

She was forced to pull out onto I-15. There was no one going south and the median blocked her view of the northbound lane. She'd have no choice but to drive that stretch of freeway back home. Hopefully the cars were cleared out of the path by now. One more hilltop and then a sprawling metropolis would great them. Her hands were slick on the wheel.

"So, what is it that you do?" Robin asked. They'd both been silent on the drive. Tessa hated that question. All the things she could have been, the degree she never finished, her father's rants about what she'd given up. It all echoed like a broken record telling her she wasn't good enough.

"I have kids," she said, expecting the typical "oh" response from a woman who wore white high heels to send her significant other off.

"How many?" Robin asked. Her voice was a little slurred. Tessa wondered if she was in shock.

"Two. A boy and a girl."

"That's fun. One of each." Robin nodded as she turned to look outside. The light from the window reflected on her blond hair, forming a halo around her head. "Joe really wants a family. We stopped trying to prevent pregnancy a few months before they left, but nothing happened."

"It will…" The words of reassurance died on Tessa's lips. There was no guarantee it would happen. There was no guarantee either of their men were coming home. "I like to make things," she blurted out awkwardly. "You know like DIY type stuff."

Robin laughed softly and the sound of Tessa's outburst hung in the stifling air of the truck. She cringed and focused on the road ahead. This was without a doubt the most uncomfortable she'd been

192

in as long as she could remember. *Just drop her off and be done with this nonsense.*

Tessa slammed on the brakes at the top of the hill. The smoke was thicker at this vantage point, choking the blood red sun and blanketing the city below with falling ash. But it wasn't the fire that suffocated her now. Thousands of people were on the freeway miles ahead of Escondido heading north on foot and spreading out for the vehicles that forced their way through the evacuating horde. They looked like ants in a colony from this distance, all fleeing from the glowing flames on the horizon over the next hill.

"It's not just the mountains," Tessa whispered.

Robin leaned forward and lifted her sunglasses. "What's happening out there?"

"I thought it was the mountains but it looks like San Diego is on fire." Tessa glanced over her shoulder, making sure she could easily turn around. "Why don't you come stay at my place? I don't think it's safe for you here now."

"I'll be fine," Robin said as she reached for the door handle. "You can drop me off here."

Let her go. You're running out of time. "Stop. I said I'd take you home."

Robin dropped her hand onto her lap and lowered her face. "Thank you."

Tessa avoided the potholes of the exit ramp that led underneath the freeway and glanced at the concrete structure above them. In a few days, thousands of feet would be pounding across this point. *Do they even have a place to go?*

"Make a right up here at the light," Robin said.

Tessa turned the wheel. "Listen, I've never been one to pry into someone else's business but you look like you got in a fight with a bus. Are these jerks still around your apartment? Do you really think you'll be safe here?"

"Turn left." Robin pointed to the road up ahead. "They're gone now. It was some kind of gang going door to door demanding food and it was my fault for putting up a fight."

"What are you talking about?" Tessa's foot hit the brake and Old Blue screeched to a stop in the middle of the intersection. Her nerves were shot and her voice was harsher than she intended. "How is this your fault?"

"Don't worry about me." Robin glanced at Tessa from the corner of her swollen eye that was partially obscured by the big sunglasses.

"I'm worried." Tessa grit her teeth.

"Don't be."

Robin's stubborn independence infuriated her and she was tired of wasting precious time away from her kids. The whole world was burning down around them and this woman was blaming herself for getting hit.

"I don't care what you think," she snapped. "It isn't safe for you here. You're coming home with me and that's final."

"My apartment is right over there." Robin pointed to the painted high-rise luxury building across the street as she pressed herself against the door, shrinking under Tessa's outburst.

She pressed on the gas, jumping over the median and driving through the open iron gate that swung on broken hinges. "Fine then. Let's go get your things."

The apartment complex, despite its manicured hedges and gazebo arched walkways, looked like something from a war-torn landscape. Dirty clothes hung draped from balconies and the pristine pool behind the cabanas was being emptied by a line of anxious tenants holding buckets. Faces were hardened in mistrust as the neighbors tried to not bump into each other and Robin wasn't the only one who looked like she'd seen the wrong side of a fist.

"Who exactly were these jerks?" Tessa eased Old Blue into a parking space.

"Like I said, some gang or something. They didn't exactly stick around and make introductions." Robin nursed the cut on her lip, hesitating before she opened the door. "I don't want to leave without my cat."

"Then get your cat and hurry please." Tessa scanned the parking lot, watching for anyone to get too close to the truck.

"She's been missing for a few days," Robin whispered. *Seriously?* Tessa whipped her head to the side to stare at the woman. Tears ran down Robin's bruised cheek as she struggled to keep herself together.

Sighing, Tessa pocketed the keys. "I'll help look for your cat while you throw a bag together, but I want to get out of here as soon as possible."

"Alright." Robin drew in a shaky breath and glanced back at the broken gate, seeming to remember where she was. "She'll be okay if we can't find her. Minerva is tough."

Tessa's heart broke for the woman. "I'll call for her. Maybe she's hanging around outside. You go get your things and hurry."

Robin sniffed and reached under her glasses to wipe the tears from her eyes. "Thank you, for everything."

The overpowering scent of smoke in the air couldn't cover up the smell of garbage that burned Tessa's nose when she opened the truck door. She tried to breathe through her mouth, but the taste of it filled her throat. Robin raced ahead, immune to the putrid assault, as Tessa cupped her hands over her face. The walkways were littered with trash and the single dumpster in the parking lot was overflowing.

Six days past a normal waste pickup in the Southern California heat had reduced the luxury apartments to this awful stench.

Tessa followed Robin through the open walkway, whistling for Minerva as if she were a dog. Every step away from the truck felt wrong, like she was abandoning her kids. It'd be dinnertime soon. Sally would feed them, but she'd owe her more food. Hopefully they weren't worried. She prayed they were okay. *What if something happens…*

"Minerva, come here kitty kitty," Tessa's high-pitched voice echoed down the walkway. Robin pulled out a lanyard from her pocket and unlocked her floor level apartment.

Tessa turned to try again. "Come here, girl. Your mama wants you." The sound of a couple arguing behind the thin walls next door was the only noise in return.

She stopped in front of Robin's open door. Trash bags were neatly piled outside, leaning against the huge mattress propped against the stucco walls. She took a step back, wondering why Robin would have dragged it outside for a garbage man who was never coming, and the realization made her sick. She didn't want to see it, but she had to know. Dark red and angry bloodspots stained the hidden side. Tessa let it fall back against the wall and put her hands over her mouth to stop from screaming. *Is this what is coming? Will Emily be safe in a world like this?*

"Robin," her voice cracked as she stepped inside the apartment.

"Did you find Minerva?" Robin turned to look over her shoulder with a hopeful smile and a half packed duffle bag on the table beside her.

"Not yet." Tessa wrang her hands.

The apartment was immaculate. Potted plants with wide green leaves sat on every windowsill. A modern couch with throw pillows that seemed as if they'd never been touched sat at perfectly squared angles on the cushions. A high fiber oriental rug without a single stain rested beneath the couch's feet. This was the home of the woman with white heels. The mattress and Robin's sweatpants and trench coat told a story that made Tessa hate the entire world.

She wanted to ask if Robin was okay, wanted to wrap her arms around her and absorb some of the hurt like she would with her kids, but Robin's sunglasses were off and she stood proudly in her own home with a look of determination on her face.

"I need to let him know where I'm going." She dug through the drawers in the kitchen. "Why don't we have any paper? I can't remember the last time I wrote a note that wasn't on my phone."

Tessa leaned back outside, thankful she had a direct line of sight to Old Blue. There'd be time for healing later, but she needed to get out of here soon and she wasn't leaving Robin behind to face the dangers of this world alone. "Write it in sharpie on the wall. Tell him you're with HM2 Ward's wife. He'll know where to find us."

Robin left bowls of food and water on the small back porch, calling for Minerva a final time and then promising she'd be back in a few days. Tessa didn't point out the obvious. The woman had already been through enough. For the first time Tessa noticed the slight limp in Robin's walk. *She hiked for miles after that.* She swallowed down the feral rage that was building inside her. It didn't matter if she was a stranger. The men they loved were together somewhere and Tessa silently vowed no one would ever hurt this woman again.

"I don't have much to offer you." Robin's shoulders hunched after she'd scanned the parking lot one more time to check for the runaway cat.

"You can help me keep a look out." Tessa shifted into drive and tried to come up with a reason to not make Robin feel like she was a burden. "I don't know if I can watch everything while taking care of the kids."

"Two kids. A boy and girl," Robin whispered as if this simple conversation was perfectly normal and the world wasn't falling down around them. Was it only a few days ago that Tessa was trying to do the same? She didn't know anymore. Everything was happening too fast.

"Mason is my son and Emily is my daughter. They're going to love having you stay with us."

The smoke thinned in the sky the further north they went on the freeway. Tessa glanced in her rearview mirror as they crested the ridge. The burnt sun in its fiery red hue distorted by the smoke hung low in the west, shining down on the thousands of people migrating in the distance behind them. She passed a group of people with their thumbs in the air, and forced herself to block out their desperation and pleading eyes. There was no way to help everyone. She wasn't even sure if she could help herself.

"Why are they staying on the freeway? Why not take a side road?" Robin wondered aloud as they passed a family setting up a tent on the shoulder of I-15.

Tessa thought about it for a minute. "I once read this article on how humans will take what they perceive as the shortest path even if it's longer. Maybe they don't know any better. Or it's possible that freeways symbolize escape." She thought back to her mistake of going to the main gate with the kids that day. "Or maybe they are doing what they've always known and sticking to the same paths they've driven before."

Robin slumped back against the seat and slid her sunglasses onto her face. "I hate to say it, but I would have done the same thing if this were to get any worse."

How much worse can it get? Tessa pressed her foot down hard on the gas pedal and willed Old Blue to move faster.

She breathed a sigh of relief as she finally got off the freeway and turned down the familiar roads. There were more cars jammed onto the interstate than she'd counted before and it dawned on her that there would be even more when everyone ran out of gas. Old Blue was almost on empty too. The gas can in the garage would help, but she needed to get more.

"Is this your neighborhood?" Robin watched the two-story houses and tidy lawns of the subdivision pass them by. "It's so quiet here. Did everyone leave?"

Tessa glanced at the closed curtains on each of the homes and shook her head. "Don't let appearances fool you."

14

"Mommy!" The screen door slammed as Emily came barreling out of Sally's house with Moose running behind her. Tessa caught the girl in her arms and buried her face against her soft red hair, inhaling her baby's scent. It'd only been half a day, but she could count on one hand the number of times she'd been away that long in her life. Moose whined, thumping his tail against the dirt and sensing something was wrong.

"Where's Dad?" Mason stood on the porch and stared past Tessa to see Robin. She hadn't told them where she was going, but he was smart enough to figure it out.

"Let's talk about that later." Arthur rested a hand on Mason's shoulder. Tessa gave him a grateful smile.

"And who's this?" Sally pushed open the door, breathing heavily as she leaned on her cane. All eyes traveled to Robin and she seemed to shrink into herself.

"This is Gunny Fuimaono's fiancé," Tessa explained as she wrapped her arms tighter around Emily and stood up. "She's going to be staying at the house for a while."

"A soon to be Marine wife." Sally nodded. "What are you waiting for, sweetheart? Come inside and get some dinner." Robin looked to Tessa for reassurance and she motioned for her to go. *One more mouth to feed.* Tessa pushed the thought away as she snuggled against Emily in her arms. She'd figure it out.

"Did you decide that you're staying then?" Arthur asked once the kids were inside with Sally and Robin.

Tessa leaned down to scratch Moose behind the ear. "No. I just haven't told her that we are leaving yet. She's been through too much already. I wanted to keep her safe and she can stay at the house if she doesn't want to come with us."

"I see." Arthur rubbed the back of his neck. "We had a little situation while you were gone."

The weight of the day settled heavily onto her shoulders. "What happened? Did the kids break something?"

"Nothing like that. A man was snooping around your yard a few minutes after you took off. I had a conversation with him, but I think things are starting to get worse."

Her cheeks grew hot with rage. "What did he say?"

"That he was coming to check on you. Neighborly concern and some other crap. I watched him walk down Turner Street and enter that house with the yellow trim." Arthur pointed down the hill.

Tessa turned to look over the hedges. "He would have seen me drive away then. I'm already worried about neighbors telling my personal business to the cops. Am I going to have to worry about them stealing from us too?"

"Do you know any of them well enough that they'd feel bad for taking what you have to feed their starving families?"

"I don't know anyone that well." Tears filled her eyes as she thought of what she would do if Mason and Emily were ever truly hungry. "We need to go. San Diego is burning and there are thousands of people on the roads heading north. I ended up in Escondido when I picked up Robin and it's bad. A gang ripped through her apartment complex and…" Her voice hitched. She couldn't say the words out loud. "They took everything they wanted. We have to get somewhere safe to ride out the worst of this until they get the power turned back on."

"If they ever get the power back on." Arthur let out a heavy sigh.

"Come with us," Tessa pleaded. "We'll take it easy and keep Sally comfortable."

"Sally is tougher than you think, but it isn't about that. She's not going to leave here without Anissa. I tried to reason with her already." The words hung in the air between them and Tessa understood. She'd do anything for her kids, even leave her home without the man she loved in order to keep them safe. But she knew the pain Arthur must be feeling in knowing the truth and not being able to convince his wife of it. At least there was a chance with Landon already being on ship. Anissa was in Germany.

"We'll talk about it later?" she offered. Arthur gave her a sad smile and nodded. They both knew later wouldn't come. Time was running out.

"Why can't she sleep with me?" Emily pouted as Robin and Tessa tucked the fitted sheet around the mattress in the guest room. Robin smiled, saying nothing. The girl had been on her lap all night.

"Because she doesn't belong to you." Tessa shoved the pillow into the case. "Now go get ready for bed."

"She's sweet." Robin smoothed out the wrinkles on the comforter. "Thank you again for taking me in. I feel bad imposing on you like this, but it feels so much safer up here somehow."

For now. Tessa shook her head. In the quiet of her house with the setting sun casting a warm glow through the window it would be easy to believe that nothing had changed that much. But she knew what was coming.

"Do you want to talk about what happened to you?"

Robin gently touched the bruising on her face and tried to smile. "Your son said it looks like I was in a gnarly fight. Gnarly. I haven't heard that word since college."

"He picks up the weirdest things from school. But I was wondering about the other stuff." She clutched the pillow to her chest, unsure of how to word it but knowing it had to be said. "I saw the mattress. I know what they did. It isn't your fault."

Robin's eyes glimmered with tears as she turned away. "It happens, you know. But no, I don't want to talk about it."

A deep motherly and protective rage squeezed at Tessa's heart, but she bit her tongue. "Alright, but if you ever need to talk then I'm here to listen."

Robin's shoulders sagged and she took a few deep breaths, collecting herself. "Thank you."

"Stop thanking me." Tessa tossed the pillow onto the bed. "I'd like to think that if I were in your shoes, you would have done the same. But to be honest, there's no way I could pull off those six-inch heels. I'd stumble around like a newborn baby gazelle." Robin burst out laughing and Tessa couldn't help but smile.

"Okay. I hate to ask because you've already done so much for me," she spoke through giggles as she tried to get them under control, "but you wouldn't happen to have any wine, would you? I could really use a drink."

"No wine," Tessa said, slightly embarrassed. A girl like Robin would drink wine but she could never stomach the stuff. "But I did stock the garage fridge with beer for Landon's homecoming." The smile fell from her face. *Landon isn't coming home.*

Robin noticed the shift immediately and straightened her shoulders, dancing a little to keep things light hearted. "Think he'll mind if we have a few?" She was weird but Tessa already liked her.

"Not at all." Tessa winked. "Let me get the kids to bed and I'll meet you out back on the porch."

"Mom, I'm worried." Mason snuggled deeper into the blanket and looked past her to the glow in the dark stars stuck to his ceiling. "Dad isn't coming home, is he?"

"We don't know that." She smoothed back the hair from his forehead. It was so long it was in his eyes. "I know in my heart that Daddy will do anything to get back to you."

"What if his ship sank?" The pain in the question sliced through her core, a million *what if* scenarios running through her brain. She swallowed back the choking fear for Mason's sake.

"It's a good thing Daddy is a strong swimmer then. He'll always find a way." Doubt plagued her, but she forced conviction into her words.

"Will Grandpa let Daddy stay with us when we go to visit him?"

"Of course he will." Tessa switched off the lantern and pressed her lips against his cheek. "Go to sleep now, buddy. We've got a lot of packing to do tomorrow."

"God, I need one of these." Tessa twisted the top off the warm beer as she slumped onto the wicker seat next to Robin.

"Me too." Robin stared at the star speckled desert sky. With no light pollution it was a brilliant thing to behold. Foam filled the neck of her bottle as she tilted it to her lips. "Want to talk about it?"

"No." Tessa shook her head. "I just want to enjoy my drink."

"Want to know something stupid?" Tessa asked as she finished her beer.

Robin pulled her knees to her chest and nodded. "A distraction would be nice right now. Tell me all the stupid things."

Tessa laughed at her eagerness and twisted the cap off her second warm beer of the night. "I have this dumb thought that this was all my fault."

"Do tell." Robin rested her chin on her knees and waited. "I want to know what you did to make the sun so mad she turned the whole world off."

"Well, when you put it that way." Tessa rolled her eyes as she took a sip.

"I'm serious." Robin reached out to smack Tessa's leg. "Tell me what you're thinking about."

"It really is stupid," Tessa groaned. "I sent an email I shouldn't have sent."

"To the government?" Robin raised her eyebrow.

"No. To Landon." A week ago, this would have seemed so trivial. But now the world was ending and those might have been the last words she'd said to him. *Don't think like that.* Her eyes welled with tears.

"I was mad. The kids were melting down. They were in port in Hawaii and he ate at some fancy restaurant with his Marines while we had cold cereal for dinner. I wrote some things I shouldn't have and now I feel like the universe it punishing me." It all came out too fast, the alcohol loosening her tongue, and she wished she could take it back.

"So you sent an email and the lights went out. Makes perfect sense if you ask me." She turned to look at the stars again. The full moon lit up her face with a soft glow. "It wasn't your fault."

"Stop." Tessa pressed a finger to her lips.

"I'm only kidding." Robin took a sip of her beer. "That's what you told me, right?"

"No, I mean stop talking." She jumped from her seat, sending the empty bottle at her feet rolling across the patio. "Did you hear that?"

"Hear what?" Robin set her beer on the table and looked to Tessa with frightened eyes.

The faint of a whisper. Someone speaking in hushed tones. The crunch of gravel under a foot. Sounds normally unnoticeable unless there was no background noise anymore. Moose started barking inside the house as he ran toward the door.

"Someone's coming." Adrenaline coursed through her veins as she ran to the house. Robin sat motionless, frozen in her chair. Tessa paused for half a second at the back door to scream, "Get inside now."

She fled up the stairs while Moose continued his low warning bark in the living room, vowing that this would be the last time her gun was ever out of reach.

"What are we going to do?" Robin pressed herself against the wall in the hallway, scared to enter Tessa's personal space.

"Do you know how to shoot?" She pulled Landon's .30-30 from the gun safe.

"No. I can't," Robin stuttered as Tessa pressed the rifle into her hands.

"Don't worry then. I don't know how to load it." Tessa slid the magazine into the pistol and racked it to chamber a round. "Just hold it like you know what you're doing while I figure this out."

Moose's barks were growing more intense as Tessa slipped through the darkness of her house but no one was near the door. She motioned for him to lay down and prayed his barks didn't wake the kids. Robin stayed on her heels, shaking with the rifle in her hands.

"What do I do if they figure out this thing isn't loaded?" Her voice was a frantic whisper in the night.

"Let's hope this is nothing." Tessa opened the front door and stepped outside. "But if it's something, use it like a baseball bat, okay?"

Robin followed Tessa as they crept along the side of the house staying as close as possible to the wall. She heard it again. A man's voice, louder this time, urgent as he gave directions.

"She parks the truck in the garage."

"Can I help you?" Tessa stepped onto her driveway with the pistol pointed in the direction of the voice. A woman gasped, clinging to the arm of the man with broad shoulders who raised the barrel of a Glock at Tessa. There were two more men with them. One had a crowbar at his side.

And the other had his hands in the air. "We don't want any problems," he said.

Tessa held her arms steady as she shifted her aim to the man with the gun. Landon's words were a dark memory in her ear. *If anything ever happens, shoot to kill. Don't engage.* The woman with the group started to cry, begging them to leave.

"If you don't want any problems, why are you on my property with a gun in my face?"

"Why don't you put your gun away and then I'll put down mine." The man took a step forward, pushing away the woman who tried to grab at the hem of his shirt.

"No thanks." Tessa shook her head, anxiety pulsing through her in waves. "And it's time for you to leave now. Go back to wherever you're from or keep moving down the freeway to somewhere else."

"You know, I've been here since long before they put this house up for rent. What's it been? Three times over the last ten years now." The man with the crowbar glanced over his shoulder to his friends as he stepped closer to Tessa. The sharp scent of hard liquor radiated from his skin. "Your husband is military, right? Where's he been? I haven't seen that truck in a while until you started driving it this past week."

Tessa tightened her grip on the pistol. Blood pounded in her ears and her stomach knotted as if she'd been punched. "I'm done talking. Turn around and get away from my house."

"Or what?" The man with the Glock stepped forward, a crooked grin spread across his face.

"Please stop, Jed. We'll take my car," the woman cried as she reached for him again.

"Or we'll blast your brains all over the street," Robin screamed as she stepped out from the shadows with the rifle aimed at Jed's chest. Her voice had just enough crazy to make him stagger back, tripping over his own feet and dropping the Glock to the ground.

"There's no need for all of this." The unarmed man took a step forward with his hands still in the air. "We have a proposition for you. My wife Charlie said she spoke with you the other day and you were a reasonable person. I have family up north in the Sierra mountains and you have a working truck. If you can get a group of us there, then I promise you'll have a place to stay. You have kids, right? I think

212

mine go to the same school. We're just down the hill on Turner Street. The house with the yellow trim."

Rage clouded Tessa's vision and her finger brushed against the trigger as she turned the weapon toward him. "So you were the one sneaking around my house earlier today?"

"Don't touch it," Robin growled as Jed picked up his gun.

Tessa aimed at Jed's chest. "This is your last warning. Get away from my property, now."

"Please, babe." Tears streamed down the woman's face and she turned to the side, exposing the wide belly that stretched out her thin t-shirt. He pushed her back when she reached for him. *I can't shoot a pregnant woman.* Tessa's hands started to shake under the weight of the pistol.

The man with the crowbar took advantage of the situation, lunging forward to grab Tessa's arm. She turned and fired at him point blank. Blood splattered her face as he fell.

"Go!" Robin screamed a feral sound as she charged down the driveway. The pregnant woman grabbed Jed's gun and started running, forcing him to chase her away. Charlie's husband bolted after them.

Tessa lowered her pistol, her heart pounding so hard it threatened to crack her ribs, and she turned to the man bleeding out onto her driveway. His fingers moved blindly against the ground searching for the crowbar and she kicked it out of reach.

"Why did you do this?" Tessa cried. The man looked to her with wide white eyes, staring straight

213

through her as the life left them. The moon reflected off the little league coach emblem embossed on his dark blue wind breaker.

Bile rose in the back of her throat and she turned to throw up on the pavement. Her vision blurred. She dropped to her knees and pressed her palms and the frame of the pistol against her eyes to make it stop.

A heavy hand laid on her shoulder. "You did good. I wasn't sure you had it in you for a second, but you took care of it."

"Were you standing there watching?" Tessa scrambled backwards with tears burning her eyes. "Oh God, what did I do?"

"What you had to do." Arthur slung the strap of his rifle over his shoulder and held out a hand to help her up.

Robin stared at both of them with her beaten face twisted in horror. "We need to call the cops somehow."

"Yes." Tessa spit the taste of vomit from her mouth and rose shakily to her feet. "This wasn't some random druggie. This was one of our neighbors. He could have been someone's father. The police need to know what happened to him. I'll drive down to the shelter in the morning to report it."

Arthur sighed, shaking his head. "How many times are you going to flaunt that giant truck driving past the houses where people are already starting to think about rationing food for their kids?"

"Is that what this is about?" Tessa struggled to fill her lungs with air. "Are bodies going to start piling up on my doorstep because I have a working truck? You have one too."

"It's not only about the truck." Arthur grunted as he grabbed the dead little league coach's arms and heaved the body over his shoulders.

"People are scared. How many of them do you think are sitting in their homes wondering what they'll do next week when the power doesn't come back on? And when it doesn't, when the reality sets in, they'll understand that no one is coming to fill the grocery stores. That the numbers they saw last week in their bank accounts, digital numbers on a screen that they spent years of hard work to build, mean absolutely nothing now. The primitive urge to flee to fertile and sustainable land will infect every sane human being that wasn't prepared for this. You're already feeling it too. And for those who don't know what to do, they're watching you drive around with something they don't have. A means to escape. As everything runs out, they're going to take what they need to survive. So, yes, I have a working truck. But there is a reason I haven't driven it."

"They're going to come back here. It isn't safe." Robin's skin was as pale as the full moon.

Tessa laced her fingers around the woman's cold hand, drawing strength in comforting her. "We're going to go somewhere safe."

"Where?" she shrieked. "This is really happening. There's nowhere safe anymore."

It was all hitting her too fast. Reality shocking her system as if she'd jumped into an icy lake. It took Tessa days to come to terms with the truth.

She ran her hand up and down Robin's arm, willing her to focus. "It's going to be okay. I have a place to go in rural Idaho and you can come with us there. It's a small town hidden in the mountains. We'll be safe until this all blows over."

Tessa cast a sharp glare at Arthur as he started to speak and silenced him. Robin had already been through too much. She didn't need to hear more right now.

"I can't leave." Robin shook her head. "What happens when Joe gets back?"

"Landon knows where we are going. He'll let Joe know too, but we can leave directions for him just in case."

"Okay," Robin whispered. She was checking out, retreating into herself. But Tessa didn't have time to try to help fix all the damage that had been done to her before they left. She only hoped that whatever crazy strength that had motivated her to rush those men with an unloaded rifle would return if they ever needed it again.

"It's time to go now." She gave Arthur a sad smile.

He nodded, shifting the dead man's weight on his back. "I don't think you have another choice."

"Attention all hands. Stand by for words from the commanding officer."

Landon placed the worn cards face down on the table, guarding the ace of spades with the palm of his hand. Every Marine's face was turned skyward as they paused their games and electronic devices. Sgt. Sierra met Landon's gaze from across the table, trying to use the moment to get a secret insight into what his teammate was holding since he'd already laid his highest spade, the ten. Thankfully, they'd bid low.

Landon smiled, shaking his head as the 1MC static filled the berthing and gave way to the commanding officer's voice. They'd been waiting for this announcement since the watch had changed shifts, spreading word like wildfire below deck that land was in sight.

"Good evening sailors and Marines. As I'm sure you're all aware of now, we've reached the coast of California sooner than expected. Communications have been down between 32nd Street and Pendleton since the beginning of the solar event. We're currently trying to establish contact with the harbormaster in San Diego to see what we can do to dock."

Landon scanned the faces of his Marines, watching their jaws tense in anger. This wasn't protocol. They normally flew and drove off ship before it completed its mission. Panic reared its head again, tightening the muscles in Landon's back. If they were this close to shore, he should already be gearing up with his unit to get on an amphibious assault vehicle.

"I understand that this is different than you are used to," the commanding officer continued. "But we need to figure out what is going on out there before we decide what to do here."

The cards grew sweaty under Landon's palm. He pulled his hand away and wiped it against his green sweatpants under the table.

"Is he saying he has no clue what's going on?" Cpl. Hemming shoved another pinch of dip into his already full lip. He cursed under his breath, hands shaking as he failed to secure the lid back on to the can.

"It's alright," Landon said stoically. "They'll let us know what's going on as soon as they find out."

But there was only so much words of reassurance could do. The stress and tension running through the berthing wrapped itself around Landon's neck.

"In about an hour, we'll be coming up to the Coronado Bridge and try to establish a…"

There was a muffled skirmish, harsh words spoken in crackled whispers, as the 1MC microphone changed hands.

"Don't you worry, Marines," COL Brown, the MEU commander, said. "We're going home one way or another. This is just a quick pit stop."

Cpl. Hemming clapped Landon on the back, grinning with pieces of tobacco stuck in his teeth as the steel walls of the ship vibrated with the loud chorus of "ooh-rahs."

Landon allowed himself to smile and sank back against his chair as he ran his thumb over the upside down ace.

"You heard the colonel." Sgt. Sierra laughed as he gathered up his cards from the table and fanned them in front of his face. "We've got another hour to kill, so let's see what you got."

The quiet pride of winning the game stuck with Landon as he made his way up the ladder well. Sgt. Sierra was more vocal about it as he swung himself between the hand rails.

"Next time let's bid higher." His anxious energy made Landon chuckle. The ship had stopped and was rocking in the San Diego waters. It might not be where they were supposed to dock, but he was so close to home he could almost taste it in the salty air as he stepped onto the flight deck.

"It was luck of the draw," Cpl. Hemming muttered behind them, but even he couldn't wipe the grin from his face.

The night air was chilly as it wound its way through the crowd of onlookers. Pinpricks broke out on Landon's skin. It was too quiet. Everyone was speaking in whispers. The inky black sky was abnormally bright as the full moon shone down on the harbor. The ship wasn't even close to being in the bay.

Hundreds of cargo ships groaned under the weight of steel shipping containers as they bobbed lifeless in the dark water. Beams of light swept out to one another, ghostly in the sea mist fog and flashing on and off in morse code. Landon stood at the rails, his hands clenching the steel bars when he saw what lay ahead of them.

The skyline of San Diego was licked in roaring flames casting a burning glow of inferno toward the night sky and sending plumes of black smoke that blocked out the stars in the east. The fire continued up the mountains, rolling over the landscape in patches like burning embers on a log.

"No, man. This isn't happening." Sgt. Sierra stepped back from the rails as he shook his head in disbelief. Someone bumped into him, shoving him forward, and he planted his feet firmly on the deck to keep from sliding.

"Everyone take a step back." Landon spun around to face the growing crowd with his palms raised. "It might not be as bad as it looks."

"Get out of my way," a panicked voice cried from the sea of faces. There was a shuffle of bodies, a break in the ranks, and a sailor flung himself over the railing.

"Man overboard!" the call rang out just as all hell broke loose. The crowd moved forward with frantic cries, clambering over each other to get a better look.

"Get away from the rails," Landon barked, grabbing shirt collars and arms blindly as he shoved them toward the center of the flight deck. Desperate eyes were wild and white, reflecting the moonlight.

"I said move." Landon pushed a shaking Marine and sent him tumbling into the crowd that caught him before he hit the deck. *Why isn't the CO calling this in?"* Landon grit his teeth as he continued to push back.

"Screw this." Someone leapt past him, jumping the railing like a hurdle. Landon reached out and caught the fabric of the jumper's thin t-shirt. The force propelled him forward and his chest connected with the metal bar.

"Let go of me." Hands clawed at his arm.

Landon struggled to catch his breath through the burning pain in his ribs, staring down at the kid with the drumsticks in his back pocket that he'd reprimanded only a week ago. "You're going to die if you try to swim this. Don't be an idiot. Grab my hand." The kid shook his head as his shirt began to stretch and he arched his body backwards.

"Someone get me a rope. Sierra!" His throat scratched as he screamed his friend's name. "Help me out over here."

"My girlfriend is out there. Let me go." The kid tore at his own shirt and the fabric in Landon's hand was weightless as the sailor plunged into the dark waters below the hull. Landon cursed out loud, throwing the remainder of the shirt into the wind.

And then he hesitated, calculating the distance to the water below and how far it was to shore. His thumb brushed gently against his ring.

A female sailor reached for the rails. He lunged to the side, tackling her to the deck.

"Let go of me," she cried as he pinned her down. "My babies are out there. I have to make sure they're okay."

"General Quarters. General Quarters. This is not a drill."

Landon kept his body on top of the frantic sailor until the fight drained from her. Boots stomped past their faces as they ran to follow orders. There were other sailors and Marines that lingered on the flight deck, coaxing people to move down below. He wasn't alone in this fight and yet, it still weighed too heavily on him.

"My babies," the sailor sobbed beneath him. He shifted his weight to the side, grabbing her wrist as he rocked back to his knees.

"You heard the CO. Get back to your station." He pulled her across the flight deck by her wrist, afraid to let go. Every painfilled whimper she uttered with every step tore at a piece of his heart and he wanted to yell, wanted to jump, wanted to shake some sense into her. *My kids are somewhere out there too.*

"It's going to be alright." He shoved her through the hatch. "We'll get off this ship soon."

Blood pumped hard through his veins as he surveyed the deck a final time. Search and Rescue boats were already being deployed. *They better find that stupid kid.* He willed himself to calm down, inhaling the salty air through his nose and pushing it from his lips. The stars hung silently above the world, watching as he turned his face to pray to anyone who was listening right now. *Please let them be alright. Keep them safe until I get home.*

GySgt. Fuimaono's deep voice boomed throughout the hangar bay as Landon slipped into formation behind the Marines who were still piling in. Anger and fear radiated from their skin in a sickening smell of sweat.

"Listen here, Marines." GySgt. Fuimaono's accent grew thicker as he flexed and pointed at the ceiling. "What just happened, won't ever happen again. You are still on deployment. You still have a job to do. Those sailors went AWOL. Do you understand me? They are a disgrace to the Navy."

That's harsh. Landon bit the inside of his cheek, keeping his expression neutral.

"I don't know, Gunny. Their families are out there."

Every head snapped to the side to see what Marine had a death wish.

LCpl Martinez stood at the front of the formation and shrugged. "I'm just saying."

GySgt. Fuimaono took two long and powerful steps until he stood towering over Martinez. The rest of the troops held their breath. Landon sighed as he stepped from the formation, ready to direct the anger to himself and protect the dopey lance corporal who was still adjusting to his meds.

"Martinez," GySgt. Fuimaono growled. "Did I say you could speak?"

"No…No, Gunny," LCpl. Martinez stuttered.

Then why are you still talking? Landon shook his head as he moved forward. The seventy-two-hour hold wasn't long enough and he didn't want another episode after what he'd already dealt with tonight.

"But you're right, it isn't fair." GySgt. Fuimaono folded his arms over his chest and took a step back. Landon froze along with everyone else. No one was expecting Gunny to say that.

"It isn't fair to their departments and units for abandoning their posts," GySgt. Fuimaono continued as he paced in front of the formation. "You think they are the only ones with families out there? We all want to go home. But if what we saw tonight is any indication of what the world is like, then I promise that your unit will become closer than family. You'll need each other to protect your loved ones. Is this something you're willing to give up?"

"No Gunny," Landon joined the loud response halfheartedly. The motivational speech irritated him despite its good intent.

"Attention on deck."

His hands formed fists at the seam of his pants as Landon stood up straight. COL. Brown marched to the head of the formation, nodding at GySgt. Fuimaono who gave him a smart salute, and then turned to face the troops.

"Parade rest."

Boots stomped against the deck as everyone widened their stance. COL. Brown looked them over. He was at least a foot shorter than GySgt. Fuimaono with graying hair and clear blue eyes, but he seemed older and weaker in this moment than Landon had ever seen him.

"What Gunny says is true," COL. Brown's voice cracked as he spoke and he coughed to clear it. His eyes hardened with a singular resolve. "But we are going home. The CO of this ship thought he could keep us as a personal security attachment to push into 32ND Street since we don't know what we we're facing. This wasn't approved by the Joint Chief of Staff. We haven't even been able to reach them. But he saw what he needed to see and realized there was no way he is going to safely dock or take us with him. I made sure he knew our mission wasn't in San Diego."

What exactly is our mission now? Even the colonel didn't seem to know or care to elaborate. Landon touched his ring. The small tear in the silicone band was a hair width wider and his irritation began to grow. Every second they spent talking felt like another second away from his family. A few of the troops coughed from the formation beside him. COL. Brown was losing the crowd. He sensed it too and didn't draw out the speech.

"Get to your berthing and gather your gear. The CO is setting course for the coast of Pendleton now. Be ready to disembark at 0500 tomorrow. Dismissed."

"This has to be some kind of joke, right?" Sgt. Sierra leaned closer to Landon, whispering so no one else heard his panic. "It was like the entire city was burning to the ground. Is the same thing happening everywhere?"

Landon pushed the rest of his personal items that were still in the locker deep down into his main pack before bunching up his extra uniforms and shoving them on top.

"Doc?"

Landon sighed as he turned to his old friend, recognizing the overwhelming fear on his face and knowing he was powerless to fix it. "I don't have any answers. I just want to get off this ship."

16

She'd packed quietly in the dark throughout the night, but in the end, exhaustion won. As soon as the first rays of the rising sun turned the black sky into a light shade of gray, Tessa settled onto the recliner facing the front door with the pistol in her hand and Moose snoring heavily at her feet. Her eyes drifted closed.

She forced them open a few seconds later when she felt someone staring at her and the slightest puff of hot breath against her cheek.

"Morning Mommy." Emily smiled as Tessa blinked her into focus. "Do you want to play dolls with me?"

"We've got a lot to do this morning." Tessa groaned as she stretched out the stiff muscles of her back. Emily frowned and crossed her arms. "No attitude. We have to finish packing so we can go to Grandpa's house."

"Grandpa's house," Emily screeched as she skipped through the living room. "I need my Barbies. I need my clothes. I need my sleeping bag."

"We need a lot of things." Tessa sighed as she picked up her notebook and read back through the sprawling list. She'd gone through most of the garage during the night, packing the camping gear into totes and securing them with bungee cords along with the unopened boxes of MREs and the rest of the food in the house packed into plastic bins. She'd stored snacks and water bottles and the rest of the ammunition under the bench seat of the truck. Each of the kid's backpacks had a few MREs and bottled water in them along with a change of clothes, emergency snacks, flashlights, and a blanket.

That part was the hardest. Tessa teared up as she'd packed the supplies into the unicorn and superman backpacks. She wanted to be prepared for everything, even leaving the truck in a hurry. And while she could carry the food herself, the thought of what might happen to her kids if they got separated made her nauseous. At least they would have some food. The worry was so strong it was suffocating. *Don't think about it anymore.* She had to keep moving. The kids needed her to be strong. And she would be.

She'd secured the water buckets with lids and loaded them into the back of Old Blue. *What if it's worse out there?* There wasn't another option. She had to make it to Idaho where her kids would be safe. Tessa forced all the negative thoughts away and focused on the task at hand.

She read through the items that weren't crossed off on her list yet. *Robin's backpack.* She heaved herself up from the recliner as Moose's tail thumped against the floor in anticipation.

"We'll eat before we go." She scratched him behind the ear. He grunted as he lowered himself to the floor and watched her walk away with sad brown eyes.

228

It'd be so much easier to open the garage door, but she wasn't going to do that again until they were ready to leave. The flashlight beam swept over the plastic bin on the top shelf. If she remembered right, it still had her old used purses and backpacks in it. Moving stickers of various colors were attached to the sides. It'd been a while since it was opened.

She held the flashlight between her teeth as she scaled the dusty shelves and then edged out the bin, grabbing it by the handle and lowering it down to the ground under her feet.

"Do you need some help with that?" Robin stood in the open doorway and peered into the darkness.

"I'm good," Tessa mumbled past the flashlight as she jumped down from the shelves and dusted her hands off on her pants.

Robin hugged herself, moving out of the way as Tessa dragged the bin inside. Her duffle bag was already packed and waiting by the front door. "Are you sure it's okay that I come with you to your family's place? I don't want to put you out any more than I already have."

"After that crazy stunt you pulled last night, you're stuck with me for life." Tessa winked, trying to make her feel more at ease. "Besides, Emily will have a meltdown if you don't come with us."

She shifted the crumpled purses that had lost their shape out of the way. The JanSport backpack from her brief stint in college was at the bottom.

Tessa shook it out and checked to make sure the zippers still worked.

"What's that?" Robin smirked.

"You need a smaller bag in case we have to…" Tessa's voice trailed off as she looked to where Robin was pointing. "I forgot about this." She snatched out the neon green fanny pack she'd worn once to an 80's themed party and adjusted the straps so it fit around her waist.

"You're not seriously going to wear that, are you?" Robin cringed.

"What? It's perfect." Tessa pulled the second magazine out of her back pocket and slipped it along with the 9mm into the pack before zipping it up with a smile. She gave it a pat for good measure. "You don't like my fanny pack?"

Robin hid her face behind her hands. "If this is the fashion for the apocalypse, I'm definitely not going to survive."

Laughter burned through Tessa's chest and she doubled over trying to catch her breath. But every time she looked at Robin, they both burst out laughing again. It was good to feel something that wasn't fear and Tessa stood for a moment with a wide grin across her face soaking the feeling up.

"What's so funny?" Mason climbed onto the barstool and rested his arms on the kitchen counter.

"Nothing." She turned to look at him, but he still wouldn't meet her eyes. The moment of silliness passed leaving her staring at her son's too long hair and wishing she could snap him out of this funk. *He doesn't want me.*

"Hey bud, can you help me out with something? We need to pack a bag for Dad so he'll have it when he meets us at Grandpa's house. Can you grab him his favorite shirts and a jacket or two?"

"I can do that." Mason nodded, his eyes filling with hope as he jumped off the chair.

"Alright." Robin clapped her hands together. "How do I make myself useful?"

Tessa chuckled, a soft and sad sound, as she looked back to her list. "Since you like fashion so much, why don't you go help the little diva upstairs shove her entire closet into her suitcase."

Tessa walked through the house a final time, closing blinds and locking windows as she looked out at the smoke filled sky and scanned the valley below. She paused at the framed wedding picture that was hanging in the hallway. They both seemed so young standing there outside the courthouse. Him in his dress blues and the rows of ribbons and medals that he'd earned too fast after his awful first tour of duty. Her with her pale pink sundress and sandals, clinging to his arm. Mason the size of a blueberry in her stomach.

She couldn't remember who took the photo. It must have been one of her friends. *Was it Danielle or Victor?* It didn't really matter anymore. All her friends had grown up and left that sleepy Idaho town, losing touch over the years except for social media likes and comments here and there. Now even that was gone. She pulled the picture from behind the glass, hung the empty frame back on the wall, and slipped it into the canvas bag along with the kids' baby scrapbooks.

"We're ready," Mason called out from the bottom of the stairs.

"I'll be down in a minute." She went back to her bedroom and sat on Landon's side of the bed, running her fingers over the quilt and inhaling slowly to prepare herself. There was only one thing left to do in the house.

The yellow legal notepad was inside the bedside table. She pulled it out and made circles in the corner of the page with the pen to make sure it had enough ink. It was going to hurt, but she owed it to him. Tears filled her eyes as she poised the pen on the first line to write one last letter to her husband.

I am so unbelievably sorry, babe. You have to know I didn't mean it. It's so stupid to think those were the last words I said, that I was tired of waiting for you.
I'd wait for you forever.
And now in some sick ironic twist of fate, I can't wait for you anymore. It's tearing my heart out to have to leave you behind. I don't even know if you're coming back.
That hurts so much to say.
Mason is falling apart. Our little boy misses you so much. And Emily doesn't understand everything yet, but she misses you so much too. I'm taking them to my dad's house. I really don't want to go back there without you, but it isn't safe for us

anymore. Robin, your gunny sergeant's fiancé, is with us. She's weird but I kind of like her.

Arthur and Sally across the street are the nicest people. Check in on them when you get back and make sure they are doing alright.

I don't know why I'm stalling. Okay, that's not true. If I can pretend I'm talking to you then maybe it will help ease this ache in my chest. I want to believe that you are okay. I don't want to be scared of what's going to happen. I don't know if I'm strong enough to keep them safe.

If you were here, you'd tell me that I am. You are the only one who's always had so much faith in me.

It's so hard to do these things without you.

I have to go now, but I want you to know that for the rest of my life, I will always wait for you.

"Let's go say goodbye to Sally and Arthur." Tessa finished securing the cargo in the back of the truck while Mason held the flashlight.

"Alright." He turned and ran, leaving her in the semi-darkness.

"Thanks," she called after him as she rushed to the door to stop it before it closed.

"I thought you wanted to get out of here fast." Robin moved out of the way of Moose as he went barreling outside after the kids.

Tessa grabbed the box of bullets and Landon's rifle from the counter. "We're going. I just want to figure out how to load this first." She motioned for Robin to keep up.

233

"I was about to head over to your place." Arthur held the screen door open as the kids and Moose raced inside. "Sally packed some goodies for you."

Tessa paused mid-step on the porch. "She shouldn't have done that. I'm taking her jars with us and came to apologize."

"Nonsense," Sally's bright voice came from inside the house. "Now you and Robin get in here so I can send you off with a proper meal."

Robin pushed past Tessa on the porch, turning to look at her when she didn't move. "What? If there's food involved, you don't have to ask me twice." Tessa smiled as she watched her go. Robin was alright.

She shifted her gaze to Arthur. "Are you sure you can't come with us?"

"We're staying here." The screen door slammed behind him and he pulled a folded sheet of paper from the breast pocket of his flannel shirt. "But I told you there were options if you decided to leave."

"What options?" Tessa leaned the rifle against the porch rail and crossed her arms over her chest, remembering the other night and the cryptic words he'd said. So much had happened in the last few days that time and memories weren't linear anymore, but she recalled his words as he carried the jars to her door.

"These are some addresses along your route. I've already been in contact with them and they know you are coming. Do me a favor and check in with them so that we know you are safe. I don't want Sally to worry. And if you do this for me, each one of those stops will have a full tank of gas waiting for you."

"Are you serious?" Tessa's eyes widened as she scanned the list. "How is this possible?"

"It pays to have likeminded friends." Arthur shrugged.

Tessa threw her arms around him, squeezing the gruff old Marine in an awkward hug. "You don't know how much relief this gives me. I was so worried about something happening on the drive and no one would know where we are. And the gas? Seriously? You are like my guardian angel or something. I don't know what I did to deserve your kindness, but thank you for everything you've done."

"Alright. That's enough." Arthur patted her on the shoulder. "Don't get all soft on me. I haven't done that much. Sally is the angel. And your journey is just beginning. Don't let your guard down and think this will be an easy one."

"I know." Tessa sighed, steeling herself for what was to come as she grabbed the rifle. "I hate to ask for one more favor, but can you show me how to load this freaking thing?"

17
Tessa

"I thought it would be more complicated." Robin ejected the rounds from the barrel onto Arthur's front yard.

The smoke in the air seemed to grow thicker and Tessa could taste it on the back of her tongue. She wasn't sure if it was getting worse or if it was all in her head, but she was ready to leave. Arthur had finished his 200ft fire perimeter and was working on her house next so he didn't have to worry about that structure catching fire. It had nothing to do with her or Landon he said.

"Yeah. I might have over thought it a bit." Tessa shrugged as she rubbed her shoulder. That rifle had a serious kick.

"Now you take this and be good for your mom." There were tears in Sally's eyes as she gave Mason and Emily each a brown plastic bag saved from the commissary and kissed the tops of their heads.

Tessa jogged over to give her a hug. Her body felt so frail under her arms, but warmth radiated from the woman. She wished there was a way to convince her to come with them.

"You have my dad's address. If anything happens and you need a place to go, come stay with us please. I'll have your jars clean and waiting for you."

"Knock that off." Sally swatted her away, laughing through the tears. "I want you to check in with us like Arthur told you to. And when Landon comes back, is there anything you want me to say?"

Tessa looked at the sky and wished she could feel the absolute faith that Sally still seemed to carry. "I left him a letter where he keeps the gun safe key. He'll find it if he comes back."

"Safe travels then. Now get out of here. You're wasting daylight." Sally nodded, deciding not to hear the *if*, and Tessa couldn't blame her. She wanted so badly to believe it too.

"Do we have everything?" Tessa glanced around the garage a final time as the kids climbed into the truck. Emily smiled from ear to ear as she clicked the lap belt around her tiny waist. The sight of it made Tessa cringe, but there was barely enough room for the four of them and Moose. The booster seat had to go.

"What about that?" Robin pointed to the Yeti cooler propped next to the beer fridge.

"That stays," Tessa said firmly. The steaks were probably spoiled. She hadn't opened it to check.

"Then I think we're good." Robin closed the passenger door and Moose settled on the floorboard under the kid's dangling feet.

"To Grandpa's house." Tessa adjusted the pillow under her bottom and gripped the wheel as she backed the truck out of the garage.

"To Grandpa's house," Emily echoed, throwing her hands in the air.

"Grandpa's house," Mason mumbled and stared straight ahead.

She left the truck idling on the street and ran up the driveway to close the garage door. The house didn't mean anything to her, it was just another residence in the long line of ones they'd lived in, but she still paused to say goodbye. All her stuff was here and she hoped it still would be if she ever got the chance to come back. *A year isn't so long...*

"Tessa!" Robin screamed as soon as the metal garage door touched the ground.

She turned slowly, her eyes locking onto Mason's frightened stare as Moose leapt from the open door of the truck, barking at the group of neighbors who were marching up her street.

"Get back here," Tessa growled as the man named Jed pointed the Glock at the dog. Moose gave a low whine, turning to look at her over his shoulder. She ripped the pistol from the fanny pack and aimed it at Jed. "I'll kill you if you shoot my dog."

"You're not killing anyone else, you psychopath." Olivia stepped from behind Jed's back, holding her cell phone in the air and recording the street.

"Mommy!" Emily screamed as she yanked against the seatbelt.

"Get them down on the floorboard," Tessa called to Robin, her eyes never leaving the angry mob. Olivia stood beside Jed. The pregnant woman was nowhere in sight. Charlie and her husband were at the edge of the group. She didn't recognize anyone else, but they all seemed to know who she was.

"Moose, get Mason," she commanded. He gave a short bark and raced back to the truck. Tessa took a step closer to her kids.

"Going somewhere?" a heavy-set man breathed out the words as he broke away from the crowd.

"The only place she's going to is jail after what she did to Carl," Olivia snarled.

"I don't want any trouble from you people." Tessa's arms remained steady as she took another cautious step. She didn't want to draw the aim of fire to her kids, but she wanted to get them out of here fast. Jed was the only one holding a gun. *If I take him out, will someone else grab it?*

"It's too late for that." The big man lunged forward just as Jed fired at her feet and missed. The gunshot rang loud in her ears as it mixed with Emily's panicked screams.

Tessa turned to the beast of a man, but he knocked her onto the pavement before she got the chance to fire off a round. She scrambled backwards, raising her arms and adjusting her aim as she squeezed the trigger. Blood squirted from his meaty bicep.

"She shot me!" he screamed through gritted teeth. Tessa was already on her feet, sprinting the last few steps to the open driver side door of the truck. A bullet whizzed through the air above her head and she ducked out of instinct.

"Stop her!" Olivia screamed.

Someone's arm caught her from behind, knocking the air from her lungs. Her kids' faces were full of terror as they stared at her from the dark floorboard of the truck and she was wrenched away from them. Moose whined, holding himself back, and crawled down next to the kids.

"Get them out of here," Tessa cried to Robin.

"Not without you." Robin slid the bullets into place and pushed forward the lever to chamber a round as the thick hand of the person holding her grabbed a fistful of Tessa's hair.

"Let go of my mom!" Mason scrambled to get out of the truck. Robin was forced to drop the rifle and use both her arms to restrain the kids.

Tessa kicked backwards as her feet were lifted in the air and she used the grip of the pistol, smashing it behind her head. The pistol connected with the assailant's teeth and sent hot fluid pouring down the back of her neck.

"Come on already. Someone get her hands," Jed commanded. Tessa arched her body, aiming the pistol down on the mass behind her and trying to squeeze the trigger. But the person turned her sharply to the right and the bullet pinged off the body of the truck.

Charlie stepped forward with a length of rope.

Then there were too many hands, too many bodies pressed against hers. She screamed and lashed out and tried to bite. The horror on their faces. Moose's frantic barks. Mason's screams. Emily's cries. She had to fight. *They need me to fight.*

The pistol fell to the road as her hands were bound together.

"What's going on here?" Arthur's voice was a beacon of hope in the chaos. The crowd of bodies parted, leaving Tessa tied and held back by a strong grip from behind that forced her to stay still. Arthur stood by the truck with his hand on his holster and the kids crying behind him.

"Nothing for you to be concerned with." Jed put the Glock in the waistband of his pants. "This is a citizen's arrest. She murdered a man last night and needs to pay for it."

"You're joking, right?" Tessa spit blood from her mouth onto his designer shoes. "You came by my house drunk, threatening me and trying to take my truck."

"That's not the way I remember it." Jed leaned in closer with a cruel grin spread across his face. "We were having a conversation and you snapped. Two sides to every story."

"I think you better step away from her, son." Arthur's hand moved to his holster.

Jed ripped out the Glock and pointed it lazily toward him, thug-like with only one arm. "What are you going to do if I don't, old man?"

Brain matter exploded from Jed's head. His body crumpled to the ground. The grip on Tessa's shoulders went slack and she jumped away, tripping over the body on the street.

"No!" Olivia fell to the ground by Jed's side and squeezed his hand to her chest. Makeup ran down her cheeks as she wailed, rocking back and forth on her knees.

"Who did this?" Arthur spoke loudly. His tone was authoritative and cold.

Tessa turned to him, confused. His pistol had never left his holster. She hadn't even heard a gunshot. Their neighbors turned to look at each other, searching for the one with the smoking gun.

"She did it." Charlie's husband pointed his finger at Robin.

"Me?" Robin cocked her head to the side and held the rifle upside down as she scrutinized it with wide eyes. "I don't even know how to load this thing."

The distant sounds of sirens drifted up to them on the hill. Normalcy in a rapidly fraying world. But nothing was normal anymore. A cold sweat broke out on Tessa's skin. She wasn't sure if the cops or the mob would be worse. *You should have left days ago. This never would have happened.*

"She must have shot him just like she shot Carl." Charlie reached for her husband.

"Like she shot me," the big man hissed, still holding his bleeding arm.

"My gun was on the ground." Tessa stared at the stupid pink and black pistol laying on the street and raised her hands in the air. "Plus, my hands are tied."

"One of you better have some answers soon." Arthur clicked his tongue, shaking his head from side to side as the sirens grew louder.

There were worried glances and heated glares as the mob turned on each other. Most of them took off running down the hill, but Olivia stayed on the ground sobbing onto Jed's shirt and Charlie stood with her husband to the side. The big man wasn't moving either.

"Let me go, I want my Mommy!" Emily bucked against Robin's arms.

"Mom!" Mason pushed past Arthur's legs. He plowed into Tessa, knocking her over, and she sank to her knees on the pavement.

"I'm so sorry, baby." She tried to wrestle her hands free from the rope as he wrapped his arms around her waist. The sirens grew louder. Red and blue lights crested the hill.

"Can you get this off of me?" Tessa turned to Arthur with her wrists in the air. Arthur shook his head, motioning with his eyes to the approaching police car.

"Why?" Tessa mouthed the word silently. There was a flash of movement above Arthur's head on the second story of his house as Sally closed the south facing window and quickly pulled the curtains shut. Tessa's eyes widened as the realization set in.

243

Arthur winked and gave her a knowing smile. The police car came to a stop a few yards in front of them.

"Everybody on the ground." Officer O'Brien used the car door as a shield, sweeping the remaining crowd over with his automatic service weapon. Tessa pushed Mason behind her back. "Hands up where I can see them." She lifted her bound wrists in the air.

"I'm hurt, officer. I need an ambulance," the big man held his arm as he cried.

"Then call an ambulance." O'Brien stepped away from the cover of the door and checked everyone for weapons as he passed them by.

"Jed!" The passenger door to the police car swung open as the pregnant woman ran out onto the street. Olivia scrambled away from the body, wiping snot and makeup from her face. Tessa started to shake as Officer O'Brien approached.

"Someone want to tell me what is going on here?"

"It was her," Olivia screamed. "She shot Carl last night and now she murdered Jed. You need to take her to jail before she kills someone else."

"Like I said, my hands are tied." Tessa's jaw clenched as she spoke. "I did shoot the guy last night when he was on my property and came at me with a crowbar. But I had nothing to do with what happened to this jerk and everything else I've done today is because you all attacked me." Officer O'Brien looked to the pregnant woman and she nodded.

"Mason, get back to the truck," Tessa whispered. He squeezed her harder, his small body convulsing with sobs and the need to protect her from the big things that he couldn't yet understand. She closed her eyes and prayed she'd wake up from this nightmare.

"Go back to your homes now," Officer O'Brien barked. *This is it.* He was going to take her to jail. *At least the kids have Sally and Arthur and Robin.* She'd fight her way out of this, prove her innocence somehow. Mason tightened his grip. Tears escaped from her closed eyes and rolled down Tessa's cheeks. She'd keep fighting for them no matter what happened. They needed her to be strong.

"I'm going to cut this rope now."

Tessa's eyes flew open. "Please don't take me to jail."

"You're lucky there is no room left." He pulled out a pocket knife and sawed through the fibers.

The binds fell away and Tessa wrapped her arms around Mason, pulling him to her chest like he was a baby again. "What do I need to do now? Should I get a lawyer? I swear I was only protecting my property last night and that I didn't kill Jed."

"If the courts were in session, if anything was working like normal, then I would say yes." He glanced over his shoulder at the pregnant woman who was standing over Jed's body stoically. "But her statement was enough to absolve you of any crime. Except lying to me. You said you didn't have a truck or a gun. I'm still curious where the husband is."

All at once, she really saw him. The man who stood before her folding the knife and tucking it into the pocket of his wrinkled and unwashed uniform. The deep bags under his eyes and the hopeless look within them.

"He's deployed." Tessa stood with Mason still clinging to her side. "He should have been back a week ago. I didn't want to lose hope."

Officer O'Brien's shoulders sagged with the heavy burden placed upon them. "I'd tell you to get to one of the shelters because I can't provide security out here for you and your kids, but they're almost full and we are turning people away. It's getting out of control. We can't help everyone anymore."

"I don't need your help. We're leaving now. I should have gone days ago." Tessa motioned to her pistol on the ground. "Do you mind if I pick that up though? I have a feeling I'm going to need it."

The pregnant woman refused to meet Tessa's eyes as Officer O'Brien covered Jed's body with a tarp. She wanted to thank her, to make sure she was okay, but the woman seemed to be struggling with whatever had prompted her to find the police and the situation she was in now. Olivia was nowhere in sight, but Tessa bet she was somewhere watching. Tessa only hoped that this would mean a better future for the mother and her unborn child. Even though the future didn't seem that promising either.

"Stay in touch." Arthur closed the driver side door after Tessa climbed behind the wheel. Blood and tears dried on her skin in the desert heat. Every bone in her body hurt and the emptiness in her chest was a numb and consuming ache, but she was determined to get out of there before anything else happened.

"Thank you again for everything and tell Sally I'm so grateful she was looking out." Tessa adjusted the pillow under her legs.

"Told you she was an angel. And she's a pretty good one too, isn't she?" Arthur whistled a little tune as he walked away.

"To Grandpa's house," Tessa whispered as Emily buried herself under her arm and Mason held his sister's hand.

"To Grandpa's house," Robin said, staring at her from the passenger seat and shaking her head in utter shock. "And please tell me your neighbors aren't as crazy up there."

18
Landon

They waited in the well deck for three hours past 0500, shivering until they got the all clear to board the AAVs. Landon kicked Sgt. Sierra's boot to wake him up as he buckled the inflatable life preserver around his waist and unrolled the rest to slide over his head.

"I'm coming," Sgt. Sierra groaned and wiped the sleep from his eyes. He jumped up and started barking orders at the other thirteen bodies that were assigned to ride with them. GySgt. Fuimaono was the last person in, manning the turret hatch seat.

"You ready Marines?" He grunted over his shoulder as he settled in.

Landon pulled off his Kevlar helmet and placed it in his lap. "More than ready."

Diesel fumes filled the darkness as the engine roared to life. The metal creak of the tracks on the ramp stopped abruptly when the vehicle drove into the water and Landon's stomach dropped at the sudden dip when it sank beneath the surface of the ocean. Time stopped and everyone held their breath, clutching their Kevlars and hoping for the best as the AAV regained buoyancy and started rocking hard with the waves.

"Worst part's over." Sgt. Sierra laughed. But tension already started to build as their bodies pressed too closely together, bumping into each other with the movement of the vehicle and claustrophobia set in. The waves were relentless and Landon pressed his feet onto the floor as he clung to the bench seat beneath him.

"I'm going to be sick." Cpl. Hemming gripped his Kevlar in his hands.

"No, man. Don't do it!" all of them began to scream at once.

"You better not puke in my vehicle," GySgt. Fuimaono turned in his seat, growling the order as Cpl. Hemming spewed liquid bile into his Kevlar. The hot scent of tobacco laced vomit mixed with the burning diesel fumes and choked out whatever breathable air that was left.

"I can taste it," the crew chief gagged from his seat up front.

"Nobody else throw up." Landon searched under the bench in the darkness for his day pack while everyone plugged their noses, trying not to gag.

"Why the hell did you put a dip in when you always get seasick?" Landon whispered to Cpl. Hemming as he felt for the right pocket of his med kit and pulled a Meclizine from the bag. "Swallow this and don't throw it up."

Weak sunlight filtered into the back of the vehicle as the crew chief and GySgt. Fuimaono cracked the hatches above them to let in some air.

"What's it look like, Gunny?" Sgt. Sierra asked. The Marines in the back all craned their necks toward the light as if they could somehow see.

"There's smoke from the east and more plumes from the mountains in the north," GySgt. Fuimaono paused, scanning the horizon. "But it looks like Oceanside and the base are still standing. There's no structural damage as far as I can see."

The troops cheered and clapped each other on the back. Landon breathed a sigh of relief as he rubbed his hands over his face. Tessa was smart. She'd have brought the kids to base if there were fires near their house. *They're okay.*

"Uh, guys," Cpl. Hemming said breathlessly as he dropped his vomit filled Kevlar onto the floor of the AAV and lifted his feet onto the bench. "Why is there water in here?"

Landon's eyes shot open. An inch of sea water pooled around his boots, mixing with the contents of Hemming's stomach as it sloshed around the metal floor. He put his hand in it and felt the current as it continued to rise.

"Gunny!" Landon shouted. "There's water in here!" The rear crew man's eyes opened wide in the semi darkness as he knelt to check.

GySgt. Fuimaono dropped down from the turret hatch, took one look at the floor, and spun around to face the driver. "Break formation! Gun it now. Go. Go. Go."

The AAV lurched forward at full speed, taking the contents of two more Marine's stomachs with it as the vehicle forced its way through the waves.

"Don't you stop!" Spit flew from GySgt. Fuimaono's lips as he screamed and turned back to the troops. "Drop your gear. Get it all off now!"

Landon unclipped his flak jacket. Swear words and gear flew around the back of the vehicle as the water continued to rise up to their ankles.

"Why isn't the bilge pump working, Doc?" Cpl. Hemming gripped Landon's arm. His flak jacket was still on and he sat there in shock.

"Do I look like a mechanic?" Landon grabbed him by the shoulders and shouted in his face. "Get your gear off so you don't sink."

Sgt. Sierra and Landon reached out, checking to make sure the troops had their life preservers in place as GySgt. Fuimaono continued his turbulent rant, "Go. Go. Go. Go."

Landon pressed his foot down. His whole body tensed as he willed the creaking machine to move faster.

The water rose midway up their calves, soaking into their boots. Landon called out what they already knew, "It's getting too deep, Gunny."

"Kefe," GySgt. Fuimaono cursed in Samoan as he slammed his fist against the metal side. "Open the top hatch. We're not going to make it."

"We're not?" Cpl. Hemming cried out.

"He means this death trap is not going to make it to shore, you moron. Now get up and push."

The heavy doors to the escape hatch groaned as all fifteen troops and the rear crew chief stood on the benches trying to force them open. The driver hit another wave, rocking the vehicle to the side, and throwing Cpl. Sequim to the floor. Landon reached down a hand, pulling her up from the rapidly filling seawater onto the bench as the metal doors parted above them.

Warm sunlight temporarily blinded him and Landon sucked in a lungful of fresh air as his eyes quickly adjusted. The water rose to the benches they were standing on and was coming in too fast.

"Go!" He didn't wait for the rear crew chief's command as he helped hoist Cpl. Hemming through the hatch. The corporal's fingers slipped off the slick siding as a wave washed over his head. White capped water came rushing inside from above as the water below continued to rise.

"Hail Mary, full of grace," Sgt. Sierra yelled the prayer in a demonic tone as he held onto Cpl. Hemming's other leg and together, they shoved the corporal outside into the ocean.

Landon turned and reached for a screaming Marine, using his knee to lift him up above the water that was already at their waists. The Marine struggled to get a grip on the hatch doors and Landon's boot slipped toward the edge of the bench.

"Got him," GySgt. Fuimaono's voice called out and the Marine was pulled from Landon's grasp. Then his thick arm reached back inside the compartment. "Give me another!"

Landon grabbed the closest body and shoved it toward Gunny's hand.

And then he grabbed another.

The pounding of blood in his ears drowned out all rational thought as he continued to push bodies up and felt them pulled away. He turned to look through the sinking vehicle and the dark water that was already at his shoulders to make sure no one was left behind. *Was it ten?* He'd lost count of how many he'd handed over.

He held his breath as he dove under and searched the back of the vehicle blindly with his hands outstretched. His life preserver tugged him back to the surface as the pull of the sinking AAV dragged at his boots.

"We gotta go, Doc!" Sgt. Sierra grabbed Landon and moved to lift him up.

Landon backpedaled, slipping off the bench and treading water as he tried to regain his footing. "Did we get them all?"

"Get out of there!" GySgt. Fuimaono let out a war cry as he thrust his hand in the water between them. Landon yanked on Sgt. Sierra's arm, pulling him to Gunny's grasp. His friend's eyes were wide as he was ripped out of the vehicle.

The water rose over Landon's head. He kicked off from the bench, propelling his body toward the open hatch that sank down to greet him.

A wave splashed over the top of the hatch, disorientating him as he reached for the opening. He held his breath and stilled his body as he waited for the life vest to guide him in the right direction. His fingers gripped at the rough edge of metal and hinges as his face broke through the surface.

Landon's uniform jerked against his neck and he was lifted from behind. He sucked in deep breaths as he hung suspended in the air with his feet dangling beneath him.

"Navy boys better know how to swim." GySgt. Fuimaono stood on the hull of the sinking vehicle and spun him around to gain momentum before tossing Landon into the cold Pacific Ocean.

Stinging cuts lashed across Landon's exposed skin as he hit the frigid water. He went under, the breath knocked from his lungs, and the sunlight filtered through the seawater above him. The life preserver pulled him to the surface and salt burned his eyes as he found the direction to land.

Fire pumped through his veins, propelling him forward with each powerful stroke until sand bumped against his knees. He crawled through the grains of earth, gripping handfuls of it as the waves beat against his back and he finally reached the dry sand of the sun-warmed beach.

"That's everyone," Sgt. Sierra's familiar voice called out as he raced down the shore, sending sand flying with his soaked boots to where Landon sat on all fours coughing up the sea.

"What about Gunny?" Landon wiped the saltwater from his eyes.

"Oh, he's coming," Sgt. Sierra said, awestruck. Landon glanced over his shoulder. The Samoan warrior grimaced in the too bright sun as he marched through the waves behind them. His face was a mask of utter contempt.

Landon laughed bitterly, digging his fingers in the opulent sand of the California shoreline and staring at the base structures in the distance. The rest of the AAV formation broke through the water as it continued its advance onto the beach and helicopters chopped through the air above them toward their landing pads.

"You alright, Doc?" Sgt. Sierra arched an eyebrow.

"No." Landon rocked back to his heels, unclipping the life preserver from his waist and ripping it from his neck. He raised his chin to stare at the sky. The sun was straight overhead shining down on them like this was any other day. "Screw this job. I want to go see my wife."

*

Dear reader,

If you picked up a copy of this book you've either been with me for my entire publishing journey or you've stumbled onto this by accident. If it's the latter, I apologize in advance for the weirdness that is to come. And if it's the first...
Ducks to avoid book flying across the room
Is it safe to come out now?

In all seriousness, I had to write this story. My husband is still active duty and this scenario crossed my mind more times than I'd like to admit. I promise to take you on a whirlwind of an adventure through this new series I'm writing and I sincerely hope you like it. If you want to know what happens next, you can get book two at the link below:
Almost There (Solar Burn Series #2)
https://www.amazon.com/dp/B09XQG7J5W

Also, sign up for my mailing list on my website to get random content and a couple of free short stories from my earlier works at:
www.heatherkcarson.com
As always, I'd appreciate your honest review. Your words help motivate me to keep writing and I look forward to every review I get.
Even the ones where you yell at me.
I love those ones so much.

-Heather

Other works by Heather Carson:

Project Dandelion Series

Sent to a fallout shelter to survive a nuclear catastrophe, a group of teenagers are the last hope for humanity. Can they survive living with each other first?

Also available on Audible!

Link to series page:
https://www.amazon.com/dp/B082QQ42TP

A Haunting Dystopian Tale (Trilogy)

"If Caraval and Grimms Fairytales had a baby, it still wouldn't be as terrifyingly whimsical as this novel. This book grips you from page one, until the very last sentence... A hardheaded and strong female lead saves the world yet again. But from Heather Carson, do we expect any less? Five Stars, Hands Down." - Kimberly Mearns, owner Ink Spill Indie Bookshop

Link to series page:
https://www.amazon.com/dp/B087Q4XTQ3

City on the Sea (Series)

Waterworld meets The Giver in this complete young-adult dystopian romance series that reviewers are calling a "must read." In the midst of this futuristic climate fiction adventure, one brave girl discovers that her world isn't what it seems and learns to stand up for herself, and to fight for the truth, no matter the cost.

Link to series page:
https://www.amazon.com/dp/B08P2D94R2

Made in the USA
Coppell, TX
21 January 2023

11492889R00152